Clotelle: a Tale of the Southern States

William Wells Brown

Contents

CLOTELLE: A TALE OF THE SOUTHERN STATES

BY

William Wells Brown

CHAPTER I
THE SLAVE'S SOCIAL CIRCLE.

With the growing population in the Southern States, the increase of mulattoes has been very great. Society does not frown upon the man who sits with his half-white child upon his knee whilst the mother stands, a slave, behind his chair. In nearly all the cities and towns of the Slave States, the real negro, or clear black, does not amount to more than one in four of the slave population. This fact is of itself the best evidence of the degraded and immoral condition of the relation of master and slave. Throughout the Southern States, there is a class of slaves who, in most of the towns, are permitted to hire their time from their owners, and who are always expected to pay a high price. This class is the mulatto women, distinguished for their fascinating beauty. The handsomest of these usually pay the greatest amount for their time. Many of these women are the favorites of men of property and standing, who furnish them with the means of compensating their owners, and not a few are dressed in the most extravagant manner.

When we take into consideration the fact that no safeguard is thrown around virtue, and no inducement held out to slave-women to be pure and chaste, we will not be surprised when told that immorality and vice pervade the cities and towns of the South to an extent unknown in the Northern States. Indeed, many of the slave-women have no higher aspiration than that of becoming the finely-dressed mistress of some white man. At negro balls and parties, this class of women usually make the most splendid appearance, and are eagerly sought after in the dance, or to entertain in the drawing-room or at the table.

A few years ago, among the many slave-women in Richmond, Virginia, who hired their time of their masters, was Agnes, a mulatto owned by John Graves, Esq., and who might be heard boasting that she was the daughter of an American Senator. Although nearly forty years of age at the time of which we write, Agnes was still exceedingly handsome. More than half white, with long black hair and deep blue eyes, no one felt like disputing with her when she urged her claim to her relationship with the Anglo-Saxon.

In her younger days, Agnes had been a housekeeper for a young slaveholder, and in sustaining this relation had become the mother of two daughters. After being cast aside by this young man, the slave-woman betook herself to the business of a laundress, and was considered to be the most tasteful woman in Richmond at her vocation.

Isabella and Marion, the two daughters of Agnes, resided with their mother, and gave her what aid they could in her business. The mother, however, was very choice of her daughters, and would allow them to perform no labor that would militate against their lady-like appearance. Agnes early resolved to bring up her daughters as ladies, as she termed it.

As the girls grew older, the mother had to pay a stipulated price for them per month. Her notoriety as a laundress of the first class enabled her to put an extra charge upon the linen that passed through her hands; and although she imposed little or no work upon her daughters, she was enabled to live in comparative luxury and have her daughters dressed to attract attention, especially at the negro balls and parties.

Although the term "negro ball" is applied to these gatherings, yet a large portion of the men who attend them are whites. Negro balls and parties in the Southern States, especially in the cities and towns, are usually made up of quadroon women, a few negro men, and any number of white gentlemen. These are gatherings of the most democratic character. Bankers, merchants, lawyers, doctors, and their clerks and students, all take part in these social assemblies upon terms of perfect equality. The father and son not unfrequently meet and dance alike at a negro ball.

It was at one of these parties that Henry Linwood, the son of a wealthy and retired gentleman of Richmond, was first introduced to Isabella, the oldest daughter of Agnes. The young man had just returned from Harvard College, where he had spent the previous five years. Isabella was in her eighteenth year, and was admitted by all who knew her to be the handsomest girl, colored or white, in the city. On this occasion, she was attired in a sky-blue silk dress, with deep black lace flounces, and bertha of the same. On her well-moulded arms she wore massive gold bracelets, while her rich black hair was arranged at the back in broad basket plaits, ornamented with pearls, and the front in the French style (a la Imperatrice), which suited her classic face to perfection.

Marion was scarcely less richly dressed than her sister.

Henry Linwood paid great attention to Isabella which was looked upon with gratification by her mother, and became a matter of general conversation with all present. Of course, the young man escorted the beautiful quadroon home that evening, and became the favorite visitor at the house of Agnes. It was on a beautiful moonlight night in the month of August when all who reside in tropical climates are eagerly grasping for a breath of fresh air, that Henry Linwood was in the garden which surrounded Agnes' cottage, with the young quadroon by his side. He drew from his pocket a newspaper wet from the press, and read the following advertisement:--

NOTICE.--Seventy-nine negroes will be offered for sale on Monday, September 10, at 12 o'clock, being the entire stock of the late John Graves in an excellent condition, and all warranted against the common vices. Among them are several mechanics, able-bodied field-hands, plough-boys, and women with children, some of them very prolific, affording a rare opportunity for any one who wishes to raise a strong and healthy lot of servants for their own use. Also several mulatto girls of rare personal qualities,--two of these very superior.

Among the above slaves advertised for sale were Agnes and her two daughters. Ere young Linwood left the quadroon that evening, he promised her that he would become her purchaser, and make her free and her own mistress.

Mr. Graves had long been considered not only an excellent and upright citizen of the first standing among the whites, but even the slaves regarded him as one of the kindest of masters. Having inherited his slaves with the rest of his property, he became possessed of them without any consultation or wish of his own. He would neither buy nor sell slaves, and was exceedingly careful, in letting them out, that they did not find oppressive and tyrannical masters. No slave speculator ever dared to cross the threshold of this planter of the Old Dominion. He was a constant attendant upon religious worship, and was noted for his general benevolence. The

American Bible Society, the American Tract Society, and the cause of Foreign Missions, found in him a liberal friend. He was always anxious that his slaves should appear well on the Sabbath, and have an opportunity of hearing the word of God.

CHAPTER II
THE NEGRO SALE.

As might have been expected, the day of sale brought an usually large number together to compete for the property to be sold. Farmers, who make a business of raising slaves for the market, were there, and slave-traders, who make a business of buying human beings in the slave-raising States and taking them to the far South, were also in attendance. Men and women, too, who wished to purchase for their own use, had found their way to the slave sale.

In the midst of the throne was one who felt a deeper interest in the result of the sale than any other of the bystanders. This was young Linwood. True to his promise, he was there with a blank bank-check in his pocket, awaiting with impatience to enter the list as a bidder for the beautiful slave.

It was indeed a heart-rending scene to witness the lamentations of these slaves, all of whom had grown up together on the old homestead of Mr. Graves, and who had been treated with great kindness by that gentleman, during his life. Now they were to be separated, and form new relations and companions. Such is the precarious condition of the slave. Even when with a good master, there is no certainty of his happiness in the future.

The less valuable slaves were first placed upon the auction-block, one after another, and sold to the highest bidder. Husbands and wives were separated with a degree of indifference that is unknown in any other relation in life. Brothers and sisters were tom from each other, and mothers saw their children for the last time on earth.

It was late in the day, and when the greatest number of persons were thought to be present, when Agnes and her daughters were brought out to the place of sale. The mother was first put upon the auction-block, and sold to a noted negro trader named Jennings. Marion was next ordered to ascend the stand, which she did with a trembling step, and was sold for $1200.

All eyes were now turned on Isabella, as she was led forward by the auction-eer. The appearance of the handsome quadroon caused a deep sensation among the crowd. There she stood, with a skin as fair as most white women, her features as beautifully regular as any of her sex of pure Anglo-Saxon blood, her long black hair done up in the neatest manner, her form tall and graceful, and her whole appear-ance indicating one superior to her condition.

The auctioneer commenced by saying that Miss Isabella was fit to deck the drawing-room of the finest mansion in Virginia.

"How much, gentlemen, for this real Albino!--fit fancy-girl for any one! She enjoys good health, and has a sweet temper. How much do you say?"

"Five hundred dollars."

"Only five hundred for such a girl as this? Gentlemen, she is worth a deal more than that sum. You certainly do not know the value of the article you are bidding on. Here, gentlemen, I hold in my hand a paper certifying that she has a good moral character."

"Seven hundred."

"Ah, gentlemen, that is something like. This paper also states that she is very intelligent."

"Eight hundred."

"She was first sprinkled, then immersed, and is now warranted to be a devoted Christian, and perfectly trustworthy."

"Nine hundred dollars."

"Nine hundred and fifty."

"One thousand."

"Eleven hundred."

Here the bidding came to a dead stand. The auctioneer stopped, looked around, and began in a rough manner to relate some anecdote connected with the sale of slaves, which he said had come under his own observation.

At this juncture the scene was indeed a most striking one. The laughing, joking, swearing, smoking, spitting, and talking, kept up a continual hum and confusion among the crowd, while the slave-girl stood with tearful eyes, looking alternately at her mother and sister and toward the young man whom she hoped would become her purchaser.

"The chastity of this girl," now continued the auctioneer, "is pure. She has never been from under her mother's care. She is virtuous, and as gentle as a dove."

The bids here took a fresh start, and went on until $1800 was reached. The auctioneer once more resorted to his jokes, and concluded by assuring the company that Isabella was not only pious, but that she could make an excellent prayer.

"Nineteen hundred dollars."

"Two thousand."

This was the last bid, and the quadroon girl was struck off, and became the property of Henry Linwood.

This was a Virginia slave-auction, at which the bones, sinews, blood, and nerves of a young girl of eighteen were sold for $500; her moral character for $200; her superior intellect for $100; the benefits supposed to accrue from her having been sprinkled and immersed, together with a warranty of her devoted Christianity, for $300; her ability to make a good prayer for $200; and her chastity for $700 more. This, too, in a city thronged with churches, whose tall spires look like so many signals pointing to heaven, but whose ministers preach that slavery a God-ordained institution!

The slaves were speedily separated, and taken along by their respective masters. Jennings, the slave-speculator, who had purchased Agnes and her daughter Marion, with several of the other slaves, took them to the county prison, where he usually kept his human cattle after purchasing them, previous to starting for the New Orleans market.

Linwood had already provided a place for Isabella, to which she was taken. The most trying moment for her was when she took leave of her mother and sister. The "Good-by" of the slave is unlike that of any other class in the community. It is indeed a farewell forever. With tears streaming down their cheeks, they embraced and commanded each other to God, who is no respecter of persons, and before whom master and slave must one day appear.

CHAPTER III
THE SLAVE SPECULATOR.

Dick Jennings the slave-speculator, was one of the few Northern men, who go to the South and throw aside their honest mode of obtaining a living and resort to trading in human beings. A more repulsive looking person could scarcely be found in any community of bad looking men. Tall, lean and lank, with high cheek-bones, face much pitted with the small-pox, gray eyes with red eyebrows, and sandy whiskers, he indeed stood alone without mate or fellow in looks. Jennings prided himself upon what he called his goodness of heart and was always speaking of his humanity. As many of the slaves whom he intended taking to the New Orleans market had been raised in Richmond, and had relations there, he determined to leave the city early in the morning, so as not to witness any of the scenes so common the departure of a slave-gang to the far South. In this, he was most successful; for not even Isabella, who had called at the prison several times to see her mother and sister, was aware of the time that they were to leave.

The slave-trader started at early dawn, and was beyond the confines of the city long before the citizens were out of their beds. As a slave regards a life on the sugar, cotton, or rice plantation as even worse than death, they are ever on the watch for an opportunity to escape. The trader, aware of this, secures his victims in chains before he sets out on his journey. On this occasion, Jennings had the men chained in pairs, while the women were allowed to go unfastened, but were closely watched.

After a march of eight days, the company arrived on the banks of the Ohio River, where they took a steamer for the place of their destination. Jennings had already advertised in the New Orleans papers, that he would be there with a prime lot of able-bodied slaves, men and women, fit for field-service, with a few extra ones calculated for house servants,--all between the ages of fifteen and twenty-five years; but like most men who make a business of speculating in human beings, he often bought many who were far advanced in years, and would try to pass them off for five or six years younger than they were. Few persons can arrive at anything approaching the real age of the negro, by mere observation, unless they are well acquainted with the race. Therefore, the slave-trader frequently carried out the deception with perfect impunity.

After the steamer had left the wharf and was fairly out on the bosom of the broad Mississippi, the speculator called his servant Pompey to him; and instructed him as to getting the negroes ready for market. Among the forty slaves that the trader had on this occasion, were some whose appearance indicated that they had seen some years and had gone through considerable service. Their gray hair and whiskers at once pronounced them to be above the ages set down in the trader's advertisement. Pompey had long been with Jennings, and understood his business well, and if he did not take delight in the discharge of his duty, he did it at least with a degree of alacrity, so that he might receive the approbation of his master.

Pomp, as he was usually called by the trader, was of real negro blood, and would often say, when alluding to himself, "Dis nigger am no counterfeit, he is de ginuine artikle. Dis chile is none of your haf-and-haf, dere is no bogus about him."

Pompey was of low stature, round face, and, like most of his race, had a set of teeth, which, for whiteness and beauty, could not be surpassed; his eyes were large, lips thick, and hair short and woolly. Pompey had been with Jennings so long, and had seen so much of buying and selling of his fellow-creatures, that he appeared perfectly indifferent to the heart-rending scenes which daily occurred in his presence. Such is the force of habit:--

"Vice is a monster of such frightful mien,   That to be hated, needs but to be seen;   But seen too oft, familiar with Its face,   We first endure, then pity, then embrace."

It was on the second day of the steamer's voyage, that Pompey selected five of the oldest slaves, took them into a room by themselves, and commenced preparing them for the market.

"Now," said he, addressing himself to the company, "I is de chap dat is to get you ready for de Orleans market, so dat you will bring marser a good price. How old is you?" addressing himself to a man not less than forty.

"If I live to see next sweet-potato-digging time, I shall be either forty or forty-five, I don't know which."

"Dat may be," replied Pompey; "but now you is only thirty years old,--dat's what marser says you is to be."

"I know I is more den dat," responded the man.

"I can't help nuffin' about dat," returned Pompey; "but when you get into de market and any one ax you how old you is, and you tell um you is forty or forty-five, marser will tie you up and cut you all to pieces. But if you tell urn dat you is only thirty, den he won't. Now remember dat you is thirty years old and no more."

"Well den, I guess I will only be thirty when dey ax me."

"What's your name?" said Pompey, addressing himself to another.

"Jeems."

"Oh! Uncle Jim, is it?"

"Yes."

"Den you must have all them gray whiskers shaved off, and all dem gray hairs plucked out of your head." This was all said by Pompey in a manner which showed that he know what he was about.

"How old is you?" asked Pompey of a tall, strong-looking man. "What's your name?"

"I am twenty-nine years old, and my name is Tobias, but they calls me Toby."

"Well, Toby, or Mr. Tobias, if dat will suit you better, you are now twenty-three years old; dat's all,--do you understand dat?"

"Yes," replied Toby.

Pompey now gave them all to understand how old they were to be when asked by persons who were likely to purchase, and then went and reported to his master that the old boys were all right.

"Be sure," said Jennings, "that the niggers don't forget what you have taught them, for our luck this time in the market depends upon their appearance. If any of them have so many gray hairs that you cannot pluck them out, take the blacking and brush, and go at them."

CHAPTER IV
THE BOAT-RACE.

At eight o'clock, on the evening of the third day of the passage, the lights of another steamer were soon in the distance, and apparently coming up very fast.

This was the signal for a general commotion on board the Patriot, and everything indicated that a steamboat-race was at hand. Nothing can exceed the excitement attendant upon the racing of steamers on the Mississippi.

By the time the boats had reached Memphis they were side by side, and each exerting itself to get in advance of the other. The night was clear, the moon shining brightly, and the boats so near to each other that the passengers were within speaking distance. On board the Patriot the firemen were using oil, lard, butter, and even bacon, with woody for the purpose of raising the steam to its highest pitch. The blaze mingled with the black smoke that issued from the pipes of the other boat, which showed that she also was burning something more combustible than wood.

The firemen of both boats, who were slaves, were singing songs such as can only be heard on board a Southern steamer. The boats now came abreast of each other, and nearer and nearer, until they were locked so that men could pass from one to the other. The wildest excitement prevailed among the men employed on the steamers, in which the passengers freely participated.

The Patriot now stopped to take in passengers, but still no steam was permitted to escape. On the starting of the boat again, cold water was forced into the boilers by the feed-pumps, and, as might have been expected, one of the boilers exploded with terrific force, carrying away the boiler-deck and tearing to pieces much of the machinery. One dense fog of steam filled every part of the vessel, while shrieks, groans, and cries were heard on every side. Men were running hither and thither looking for their wives, and women wore flying about in the wildest confusion seeking for their husbands. Dismay appeared on every countenance.

The saloons and cabins soon looked more like hospitals than anything else; but by this time the Patriot had drifted to the shore, and the other steamer had come alongside to render assistance to the disabled boat. The killed and wounded (nineteen in number) were put on shore, and the Patriot, taken in tow by the Washington, was once more on her journey.

It was half-past twelve, and the passengers, instead of retiring to their berths, once more assembled at the gambling-tables. The practice of gambling on the western waters has long been a source of annoyance to the more moral persons who travel on our great rivers. Thousands of dollars often change owners during a passage from St. Louis or Louisville to New Orleans, on a Mississippi steamer. Many men are completely ruined on such occasions, and duels are often the consequence.

"Go call my boy, steward," said Mr. Jones, as he took his cards one by one from the table.

In a few minutes a fine-looking, bright-eyed mulatto boy, apparently about sixteen years of age, was standing by his master's side at the table.

"I am broke, all but my boy," said Jones, as he ran his fingers through his cards; "but he is worth a thousand dollars, and I will bet the half of him."

"I will call you," said Thompson, as he laid five hundred dollars at the feet of the boy, who was standing, on the table, and at the same time throwing down his cards before his adversary.

"You have beaten me," said Jones; and a roar of laughter followed from the other gentleman as poor Joe stepped down from the table.

"Well, I suppose I owe you half the nigger," said Thompson, as he took hold of Joe and began examining his limbs.

"Yes," replied Jones, "he is half yours. Let me have five hundred dollars, and I will give you a bill of sale of the boy."

"Go back to your bed," said Thompson to his chattel, "and remember that you now belong to me."

The poor slave wiped the tears from his eyes, as, in obedience, he turned to leave the table.

"My father gave me that boy," said Jones, as he took the money, "and I hope, Mr. Thompson, that you will allow me to redeem him."

"Most certainly, Sir," replied Thompson. "Whenever you hand over the cool thousand the negro is yours."

Next morning, as the passengers were assembling in the cabin and on deck and while the slaves were running about waiting on or looking for their masters, poor Joe was seen entering his new master's stateroom, boots in hand.

"Who do you belong to?" inquired a gentleman of an old negro, who passed along leading a fine Newfoundland dog which he had been feeding.

"When I went to sleep las' night," replied the slave, "I 'longed to Massa Carr; but he bin gamblin' all night an' I don't know who I 'longs to dis mornin'."

Such is the uncertainty of a slave's life. He goes to bed at night the pampered servant of his young master, with whom he has played in childhood, and who would not see his slave abused under any consideration, and gets up in the morning the property of a man whom he has never before seen.

To behold five or six tables in the saloon of a steamer, with half a dozen men playing cards at each, with money, pistols, and bowie-knives spread in splendid confusion before them, is an ordinary thing on the Mississippi River.

CHAPTER V
THE YOUNG MOTHER.

On the fourth morning, the Patriot landed at Grand Gulf, a beautiful town on the left bank of the Mississippi. Among the numerous passengers who came on board at Rodney was another slave-trader, with nine human chattels which he was conveying to the Southern market. The passengers, both ladies and gentlemen, were startled at seeing among the new lot of slaves a woman so white as not to be distinguishable from the other white women on board. She had in her arms a child so white that no one would suppose a drop of African blood flowed through its blue veins.

No one could behold that mother with her helpless babe, without feeling that God would punish the oppressor. There she sat, with an expressive and intellectual forehead, and a countenance full of dignity and heroism, her dark golden locks rolled back from her almost snow-white forehead and floating over her swelling bosom. The tears that stood in her mild blue eyes showed that she was brooding over sorrows and wrongs that filled her bleeding heart.

The hearts of the passers-by grew softer, while gazing upon that young mother as she pressed sweet kisses on the sad, smiling lips of the infant that lay in her lap. The small, dimpled hands of the innocent creature were slyly hid in the warm bosom on which the little one nestled. The blood of some proud Southerner, no doubt, flowed through the veins of that child.

When the boat arrived at Natches, a rather good-looking, genteel-appearing man came on board to purchase a servant. This individual introduced himself to Jennings as the Rev. James Wilson. The slave-trader conducted the preacher to the deck-cabin, where he kept his slaves, and the man of God, after having some questions answered, selected Agnes as the one best suited to his service.

It seemed as if poor Marion's heart would break when she found that she was to be separated from her mother. The preacher, however, appeared to be but little moved by their sorrow, and took his newly-purchased victim on shore. Agnes begged him to buy her daughter, but he refused, on the ground that he had no use for her.

During the remainder of the passage, Marion wept bitterly.

After a ran of a few hours, the boat stopped at Baton Rouge, where an additional number of passengers were taken on board, among whom were a number of persons who had been attending the races at that place. Gambling and drinking were now the order of the day.

The next morning, at ten o'clock, the boat arrived at New Orleans where the passengers went to their hotels and homes, and the negroes to the slave-pens.

Lizzie, the white slave-mother, of whom we have already spoken, created as much of a sensation by the fairness of her complexion and the alabaster whiteness of her child, when being conveyed on shore at New Orleans, as she had done when brought on board at Grand Gulf. Every one that saw her felt that slavery in the Southern States was not confined to the negro. Many had been taught to think that slavery was a benefit rather than an injury, and those who were not opposed to the institution before, now felt that if whites were to become its victims, it was time at least that some security should be thrown around the Anglo-Saxon to gave him from this servile and degraded position.

CHAPTER VI
THE SLAVE-MARKET.

Not far from Canal Street, in the city of New Orleans, stands a large two-story, flat building, surrounded by a stone wall some twelve feet high, the top of which is covered with bits of glass, and so constructed as to prevent even the possibility of any one's passing over it without sustaining great injury. Many of the rooms in this building resemble the cells of a prison, and in a small apartment near the "office" are to be seen any number of iron collars, hobbles, handcuffs, thumbscrews, cowhides, chains, gags, and yokes.

A back-yard, enclosed by a high wall, looks something like the playground attached to one of our large New England schools, in which are rows of benches and swings. Attached to the back premises is a good-sized kitchen, where, at the time of which we write, two old negresses were at work, stewing, boiling, and baking, and occasionally wiping the perspiration from their furrowed and swarthy brows.

The slave-trader, Jennings, on his arrival at New Orleans, took up his quarters here with his gang of human cattle, and the morning after, at 10 o'clock, they were exhibited for sale. First of all came the beautiful Marion, whose pale countenance and dejected look told how many sad hours she had passed since parting with her mother at Natchez. There, too, was a poor woman who had been separated from her husband; and another woman, whose looks and manners were expressive of deep anguish, sat by her side. There was "Uncle Jeems," with his whiskers off, his face shaven clean, and the gray hairs plucked out ready to be sold for ten years younger than he was. Toby was also there, with his face shaven and greased, ready for inspection.

The examination commenced, and was carried on in such a manner as to shock the feelings of anyone not entirely devoid of the milk of human kindness.

"What are you wiping your eyes for?" inquired a fat, red-faced man, with a white hat set on one side of his head and a cigar in his mouth, of a woman who sat on one of the benches.

"Because I left my man behind."

"Oh, if I buy you, I will furnish you with a better man than you left. I've got lots of young bucks on my farm."

"I don't want and never will have another man," replied the woman.

"What's your name?" asked a man in a straw hat of a tall negro who stood with his arms folded across his breast, leaning against the wall.

"My name is Aaron, sar."

"How old are you?"

"Twenty-five."

"Where were you raised?"

"In ole Virginny, sar."

"How many men have owned you?"

"Four."

"Do you enjoy good health?"

"Yes, sar."

"How long did you live with your first owner?"

"Twenty years."

"Did you ever run away?"

"No, sar."

"Did you ever strike your master?"

"No, sar."

"Were you ever whipped much?"

"No, sar; I s'pose I didn't deserve it, sar."

"How long did you live with your second master?"

"Ten years, sar."

"Have you a good appetite?"

"Yes, sar."

"Can you eat your allowance?"

"Yes, sar,--when I can get it."

"Where were you employed in Virginia?"

"I worked de tobacker fiel'."

"In the tobacco field, eh?"

"Yes, sar."

"How old did you say you was?"

"Twenty-five, sar, nex' sweet-'tater-diggin' time."

"I am a cotton-planter, and if I buy you, you will have to work in the cotton-field. My men pick one hundred and fifty pounds a day, and the women one hundred and forty pounds; and those who fail to perform their task receive five stripes for each pound that is wanting. Now, do you think you could keep up with the rest of the hands?"

"I' don't know sar but I 'specs I'd have to."

"How long did you live with your third master?"

"Three years, sar."

"Why, that makes you thirty-three. I thought you told me you were only twenty-five?"

Aaron now looked first at the planter, then at the trader, and seemed perfectly bewildered. He had forgotten the lesson given him by Pompey relative to his age; and the planter's circuitous questions--doubtless to find out the slave's real age--had thrown the negro off his guard.

"I must see your back, so as to know how much you have been whipped, before I think of buying."

Pompey, who had been standing by during the examination, thought that his services were now required, and, stepping forth with a degree of officiousness, said to Aaron,--

"Don't you hear de gemman tell you he wants to 'zamin you. Cum, unharness yo'seff, ole boy, and don't be standin' dar."

Aaron was soon examined, and pronounced "sound;" yet the conflicting statement about his age was not satisfactory.

Fortunately for Marion, she was spared the pain of undergoing such an examination. Mr. Cardney, a teller in one of the banks, had just been married, and wanted a maid-servant for his wife, and, passing through the market in the early part of the day, was pleased with the young slave's appearance, and his dwelling the quadroon found a much better home than often falls to the lot of a slave sold in the New Orleans market.

CHAPTER VII
THE SLAVE-HOLDING PARSON.

The Rev. James Wilson was a native of the State of Connecticut where he was educated for the ministry in the Methodist persuasion. His father was a strict follower of John Wesley, and spared no pains in his son's education, with the hope that he would one day be as renowned as the leader of his sect. James had scarcely finished his education at New Haven, when he was invited by an uncle, then on a visit to his father, to spend a few months at Natchez in Mississippi. Young Wilson accepted his uncle's invitation, and accompanied him to the South. Few Young men, and especially clergymen, going fresh from college to the South, but are looked upon as geniuses in a small way, and who are not invited to all the parties in the neighborhood. Mr. Wilson was not an exception to this rule. The society into which he was thrown, on his arrival at Natchez, was too brilliant for him not to be captivated by it, and, as might have been expected, he succeeded in captivating a plantation with seventy slaves if not the heart of the lady to whom it belonged.

Added to this, he became a popular preacher, and had a large congregation with a snug salary. Like other planters, Mr. Wilson confided the care of his farm to Ned Huckelby, an overseer of high reputation in his way.

The Poplar Farm, as it was called, was situated in a beautiful valley, nine miles from Natchez, and near the Mississippi River. The once unshorn face of nature had given way, and the farm now blossomed with a splendid harvest. The neat cottage stood in a grove, where Lombardy poplars lift their tops almost to prop the skies, where the willow, locust and horse-chestnut trees spread forth their branches, and flowers never ceased to blossom.

This was the parson's country residence, where the family spent only two months during the year. His town residence was a fine villa, seated on the brow of a hill at the edge of the city.

It was in the kitchen of this house that Agnes found her new home. Mr. Wilson was every inch a democrat, and early resolved that "his people," as he called his slaves should be well-fed and not over-worked, and therefore laid down the law and gospel to the overseer as well as to the slaves. "It is my wish," said he to Mr. Carlingham, an old school-fellow who was spending a few days with him,--"It is my wish that a new system be adopted on the plantations in this State. I believe that the sons of Ham should have the gospel, and I intend that mine shall have it. The gospel is calculated to make mankind better and none should be without it."

"What say you," said Carlingham, "about the right of man to his liberty?"

"Now, Carlingham, you have begun to harp again about men's rights. I really wish that you could see this matter as I do."'

"I regret that I cannot see eye to eye with you," said Carlingham. "I am a disciple of Rousseau, and have for years made the rights of man my study, and I must confess to you that I see no difference between white and black, as it regards liberty."

"Now, my dear Carlingham, would you really have the negroes enjoy the same rights as ourselves?"

"I would most certainly. Look at our great Declaration of Independence! look even at the Constitution of our own Connecticut and see what is said in these about liberty."

"I regard all this talk about rights as mere humbug. The Bible is older than the Declaration of Independence, and there I take my stand."

A long discussion followed, in which both gentlemen put forth their peculiar ideas with much warmth of feeling.

During this conversation, there was another person in the room, seated by the window, who, although at work, embroidering a fine collar, paid minute attention to what was said. This was Georgiana, the only daughter of the parson, who had but just returned from Connecticut, where she had finished her education. She had had the opportunity of contrasting the spirit of Christianity and liberty in New England with that of slavery in her native State, and had learned to feel deeply for the injured negro. Georgiana was in her nineteenth year, and had been much benefited by her residence of five years at the North. Her form was tall and graceful, her features regular and well-defined, and her complexion was illuminated by the freshness of youth, beauty, and health.

The daughter differed from both the father and visitor upon the subject which they had been discussing; and as soon as an opportunity offered, she gave it as her opinion that the Bible was both the bulwark of Christianity and of liberty. With a smile she said,--

"Of course, papa will overlook my difference with him, for although I am a native of the South, I am by education and sympathy a Northerner." Mr. Wilson laughed, appearing rather pleased than otherwise at the manner in which his daughter had expressed herself. From this Georgiana took courage and continued,--

"'Thou shalt love thy neighbor as thyself.' This single passage of Scripture should cause us to have respect for the rights of the slave. True Christian love is of an enlarged and disinterested nature. It loves all who love the Lord Jesus Christ in sincerity, without regard to color or condition."

"Georgiana, my dear, you are an abolitionist,--your talk is fanaticism!" said Mr. Wilson, in rather a sharp tone; but the subdued look of the girl and the presence of Carlingham caused him to soften his language.

Mr. Wilson having lost his wife by consumption, and Georgiana being his only child, he loved her too dearly to say more, even if he felt disposed. A silence followed this exhortation from the young Christian, but her remarks had done a noble work. The father's heart was touched, and the sceptic, for the first time, was viewing Christianity in its true light.

CHAPTER VIII
A NIGHT IN THE PARSON'S KITCHEN.

Besides Agnes, whom Mr. Wilson had purchased from the slave-trader, Jennings, he kept a number of house-servants. The chief one of these was Sam, who must be regarded as second only to the parson himself. If a dinner-party was in contemplation, or any company was to be invited, after all the arrangements had been talked over by the minister and his daughter. Sam was sure to be consulted on, the subject by "Miss Georgy," as Miss Wilson was called by all the servants. If furniture, crockery, or anything was to be purchased, Sam felt that he had been slighted if his opinion was not asked. As to the marketing, he did it all. He sat at the head of the servants' table in the kitchen, and was master of the ceremonies. A single look from him was enough to silence any conversation or noise among the servants in the kitchen or in any other part of the premises.

There is in the Southern States a great amount of prejudice in regard to color, even among the negroes themselves. The nearer the negro or mulatto approaches to the white, the more he seems to feel his superiority over those of a darker hue. This is no doubt the result of the prejudice that exists on the part of the whites against both the mulattoes and the blacks.

Sam was originally from Kentucky, and through the instrumentality of one of his young masters, whom he had to take to school, he had learned to read so as to be well understood, and, owing to that fact, was considered a prodigy, not only among his own master's slaves, but also among those of the town who knew him. Sam had a great wish to follow in the footsteps of his master and be a poet, and was therefore often heard singing doggerels of his own composition.

But there was one drawback to Sam, and that was his color. He was one of the blackest of his race. This he evidently regarded as a great misfortune; but he endeavored to make up for it in dress. Mr. Wilson kept his house servants well dressed, and as for Sam, he was seldom seen except in a ruffled shirt. Indeed, the washerwoman feared him more than any one else in the house.

Agnes had been inaugurated chief of the kitchen department, and had a general supervision of the household affairs. Alfred, the coachman, Peter, and Hetty made up the remainder of the house-servants. Besides these, Mr. Wilson owned eight slaves who were masons. These worked in the city. Being mechanics, they were let out to greater advantage than to keep them on the farm.

Every Sunday evening, Mr. Wilson's servants, including the bricklayers, assembled in the kitchen, where the events of the week were fully discussed and commented upon. It was on a Sunday evening, in the month of June, that there was a party at Mr. Wilson's house, and, according to custom in the Southern States, the ladies had their maidservants with them. Tea had been served in "the house," and the servants, including the strangers, had taken their seats at the table in the kitchen. Sam, being a "single gentleman," was unusually attentive to the ladies on this occasion. He seldom let a day pass without spending an hour or two in combing and brushing his "har." He had an idea that fresh butter was better for his hair than any other kind of grease, and therefore on churning days half a pound of butter had always to be taken out before it was salted. When he wished to appear to great advantage, he would grease his face to make it "shiny." Therefore, on the evening of the party, when all the servants were at the table, Sam cut a big figure. There he sat, with his wool well combed and buttered, face nicely greased, and his ruffles extending five or six inches from his bosom. The parson in his drawing-room did not make a more imposing appearance than did his servant on this occasion.

"I is bin had my fortune tole last Sunday night," said Sam, while helping one of the girls.

"Indeed!" cried half a dozen voices.

"Yes," continued he; "Aunt Winny tole me I's to hab de prettiest yallah gal in de town, and dat I's to be free!"

All eyes were immediately turned toward Sally Johnson, who was seated near Sam.

"I 'specs I see somebody blush at dat remark," said Alfred.

"Pass dem pancakes an' 'lasses up dis way, Mr. Alf, and none ob your sinuwashuns here," rejoined Sam.

"Dat reminds me," said-Agnes, "dat Dorcas Simpson is gwine to git married."

"Who to, I want to know?" inquired Peter.

"To one of Mr. Darby's field-hands," answered Agnes.

"I should tink dat gal wouldn't frow herseff away in dat ar way," said Sally; "She's good lookin' 'nough to git a house-servant, and not hab to put up wid a field-nigger."

"Yes," said Sam, "dat's a werry unsensible remark ob yourn, Miss Sally. I admires your judgment werry much, I 'sures you. Dar's plenty ob susceptible an' well-dressed house-serbants dat a gal ob her looks can git widout takin' up wid dem common darkies."

The evening's entertainment concluded by Sam relating a little of his own experience while with his first master, in old Kentucky. This master was a doctor, and had a large practice among his neighbors, doctoring both masters and slaves. When Sam was about fifteen years old, his master set him to grinding up ointment and making pills. As the young student grew older and became more practised in his profession, his services were of more importance to the doctor. The physician having a good business, and a large number of his patients being slaves,--the most of whom had to call on the doctor when ill,--he put Sam to bleeding, pulling teeth, and administering medicine to the slaves. Sam soon acquired the name among the slaves of the "Black Doctor." With this appellation he was delighted; and no regular physician could have put on more airs than did the black doctor when his services were required. In bleeding, he must have more bandages, and would rub and smack the arm more than the doctor would have thought of.

Sam was once seen taking out a tooth for one of his patients, and nothing appeared more amusing. He got the poor fellow down on his back, and then getting astride of his chest, he applied the turnkeys and pulled away for dear life. Unfortunately, he had got hold of the wrong tooth, and the poor man screamed as loud as he could; but it was to no purpose, for Sam had him fast, and after a pretty severe tussle out came the sound grinder. The young doctor now saw his mistake, but consoled himself with the thought that as the wrong tooth was out of the way, there was more room to get at the right one.

Bleeding and a dose of calomel were always considered indispensable by the "old boss," and as a matter of course, Sam followed in his footsteps.

On one occasion the old doctor was ill himself, so as to be unable to attend to his patients. A slave, with pass in hand, called to receive medical advice, and the master told Sam to examine him and see what he wanted. This delighted him beyond measure, for although he had been acting his part in the way of giving out medicine as the master ordered it, he had never been called upon by the latter to examine a patient, and this seemed to convince him after all that he was no sham doctor. As might have been expected, he cut a rare figure in his first examination. Placing himself directly opposite his patient, and folding his arms across his breast, looking very knowingly, he began,--

"What's de matter wid you?"

"I is sick."

"Where is you sick?"

"Here," replied the man, putting his hand upon his stomach.

"Put out your tongue," continued the doctor.

The man ran out his tongue at full length.

"Let me feel your pulse;" at the same time taking his patient's hand in his, and placing his fingers upon his pulse, he said,--

"Ah! your case is a bad one; ef I don't do something for you, and dat pretty quick, you'll be a gone coons and dat's sartin."

At this the man appeared frightened, and inquired what was the matter with him, in answer to which Sam said,

"I done told dat your case is a bad one, and dat's enuff."

On Sam's returning to his master's bedside, the latter said,

"Well, Sam, what do you think is the matter with him?"

"His stomach is out ob order, sar," he replied.

"What do you think had better be done for him?"

"I tink I'd better bleed him and gib him a dose ob calomel," returned Sam.

So, to the latter's gratification, the master let him have his own way.

On one occasion, when making pills and ointment, Sam made a great mistake. He got the preparations for both mixed together, so that he could not legitimately make either. But fearing that if he threw the stuff away, his master would flog him, and being afraid to inform his superior of the mistake, he resolved to make the whole batch of pill and ointment stuff into pills. He well knew that the powder over the pills would hide the inside, and the fact that most persons shut their eyes when taking such medicine led the young doctor to feel that all would be right in the end. Therefore Sam made his pills, boxed them up, put on the labels, and placed them in a conspicuous position on one of the shelves.

Sam felt a degree of anxiety about his pills, however. It was a strange mixture, and he was not certain whether it would kill or cure; but he was willing that it should be tried. At last the young doctor had his vanity gratified. Col. Tallen, one of Dr. Saxondale's patients, drove up one morning, and Sam as usual ran out to the gate to hold the colonel's horse.

"Call your master," said the colonel; "I will not get out."

The doctor was soon beside the carriage, and inquired about the health of his patient. After a little consultation, the doctor returned to his office, took down a box of Sam's new pills, and returned to the carriage.

"Take two of these every morning and night," said the doctor, "and if you don't feel relieved, double the dose."

"Good gracious," exclaimed Sam in an undertone, when he heard his master tell the colonel how to take the pills.

It was several days before Sam could learn the result of his new medicine. One afternoon, about a fortnight after the colonel's visit Sam saw his master's patient riding up to the gate on horseback. The doctor happened to be in the yard, and met the colonel and said,--

"How are you now?"

"I am entirely recovered," replied the patient. "Those pills of yours put me on my feet the next day."

"I knew they would," rejoined the doctor.

Sam was near enough to hear the conversation, and was delighted beyond description. The negro immediately ran into the kitchen, amongst his companions, and commenced dancing.

"What de matter wid you?" inquired the cook.

"I is de greatest doctor in dis country," replied Sam. "Ef you ever get sick, call on me. No matter what ails you, I is de man dat can cure you in no time. If you do hab de backache, de rheumaties, de headache, de coller morbus, fits, er any ting else, Sam is de gentleman dat can put you on your feet wid his pills."

For a long time after, Sam did little else than boast of his skill as a doctor.

We have said that the black doctor was full of wit and good sense. Indeed, in that respect, he had scarcely an equal in the neighborhood. Although his master resided some little distance out of the city, Sam was always the first man in all the negro balls and parties in town. When his master could give him a pass, he went, and when he did not give him one, he would steal away after his master had retired, and run the risk of being taken up by the night-watch. Of course, the master never knew anything of the absence of the servant at night without permission. As the negroes at these parties tried to excel each other in the way of dress, Sam was often at a loss to make that appearance that his heart desired, but his ready wit ever helped him in this. When his master had retired to bed at night, it was the duty of Sam to put out the lights, and take out with him his master's clothes and boots, and leave them in the office until morning, and then black the boots, brush the clothes, and return them to his master's room.

Having resolved to attend a dress-ball one night, without his master's permission, and being perplexed for suitable garments, Sam determined to take his master's. So, dressing himself in the doctor's clothes even to his boots and hat, off the negro started for the city. Being well acquainted with the usual walk of the patrols he found no difficulty in keeping out of their way. As might have been expected, Sam was the great gun with the ladies that night.

The next morning, Sam was back home long before his master's time for rising, and the clothes were put in their accustomed place. For a long time Sam had no difficulty in attiring himself for parties; but the old proverb that "It is a long lane that has no turning," was verified in the negro's case. One stormy night, when the rain was descending in torrents, the doctor heard a rap at his door. It was customary with him, when called up at night to visit a patient, to ring for Sam. But this time, the servant was nowhere to be found. The doctor struck a light and looked for clothes; they too, were gone.--It was twelve o'clock, and the doctor's clothes, hat, boots, and even his watch, were nowhere to be found. Here was a pretty dilemma for a doctor to be in. It was some time before the physician could fit himself out so as to mike the visit. At last, however, he started with one of the farm-horses, for Sam had taken the doctor's best saddle-horse. The doctor felt sure that the negro had robbed him, and was on his way to Canada; but in this he was mistaken. Sam had gone to the city to attend a ball, and had decked himself out in his master's best suit. The physician returned before morning, and again retired to bed but with little hope of sleep, for his thoughts were with his servant and horse. At six o'clock, in walked Sam with his master's clothes, and the boots neatly blacked. The watch was placed on the shelf, and the hat in its place. Sam had not met any of the servants, and was therefore entirely ignorant of what had occurred during his absence.

"What have you been about, sir, and where was you last night when I was called?" said the doctor.

"I don't know, sir. I 'spose I was asleep," replied Sam.

But the doctor was not to be so easily satisfied, after having been put to so much trouble in hunting up another suit without the aid of Sam. After breakfast, Sam was taken into the barn, tied up, and severely flogged with the cat, which brought from him the truth concerning his absence the previous night. This forever put an end to his fine appearance at the negro parties. Had not the doctor been one of the most indulgent of masters, he would not have escaped with merely a severe whipping.

As a matter of course, Sam had to relate to his companions that evening in Mr. Wilson's kitchen all his adventures as a physician while with his old master.

CHAPTER IX
THE MAN OF HONOR.

Augustine Cardinay, the purchaser of Marion, was from the Green Mountains of Vermont, and his feelings were opposed to the holding of slaves; but his young wife persuaded him in into the idea that it was no worse to own a slave than to hire one and pay the money to another. Hence it was that he had been induced to purchase Marion.

Adolphus Morton, a young physician from the same State, and who had just commenced the practice of his profession in New Orleans, was boarding with Cardinay when Marion was brought home. The young physician had been in New Orleans but a very few weeks, and had seen but little of slavery. In his own mountain-home, he had been taught that the slaves of the Southern States were negroes, and if not from the coast of Africa, the descendants of those who had been imported. He was unprepared to behold with composure a beautiful white girl of sixteen in the degraded position of a chattel slave.

The blood chilled in his young heart as he heard Cardinay tell how, by bantering with the trader, he had bought her two hundred dollars less than he first asked. His very looks showed that she had the deepest sympathies of his heart.

Marion had been brought up by her mother to look after the domestic concerns of her cottage in Virginia, and well knew how to perform the duties imposed upon her. Mrs. Cardinay was much pleased with her new servant, and often mentioned her good qualities in the presence of Mr. Morton.

After eight months acquaintance with Marion, Morton's sympathies ripened into love, which was most cordially reciprocated by the friendless and injured child of sorrow. There was but one course which the young man could honorably pursue, and that was to purchase Marion and make her his lawful wife; and this he did immediately, for he found Mr. and Mrs. Cardinay willing to second his liberal intentions.

The young man, after purchasing Marion from Cardinay, and marrying her, took lodgings in another part of the city. A private teacher was called in, and the young wife was taught some of those accomplishments so necessary for one taking a high position in good society.

Dr. Morton soon obtained a large and influential practice in his profession, and with it increased in wealth; but with all his wealth he never owned a slave. Probably the fact that he had raised his wife from that condition kept the hydra-headed system continually before him. To the credit of Marion be it said, she used every means to obtain the freedom of her mother, who had been sold to Parson Wilson, at Natchez. Her efforts, however, had come too late; for Agnes had died of a fever before the arrival of Dr. Morton's agent.

Marion found in Adolphus Morton a kind and affectionate husband; and his wish to purchase her mother, although unsuccessful, had doubly endeared him to her. Ere a year had elapsed from the time of their marriage, Mrs. Morton presented her husband with a lovely daughter, who seemed to knit their hearts still closer together. This child they named Jane; and before the expiration of the second year, they were blessed with another daughter, whom they named Adrika.

These children grew up to the ages of ten and eleven, and were then sent to the North to finish their education, and receive that refinement which young ladies cannot obtain in the Slave States.

CHAPTER X
THE QUADROON'S HOME

A few miles out of Richmond is a pleasant place, with here and there a beautiful cottage surrounded by trees so as scarcely to be seen. Among these was one far retired from the public roads, and almost hidden among the trees. This was the spot that Henry Linwood had selected for Isabella, the eldest daughter of Agnes. The young man hired the house, furnished it, and placed his mistress there, and for many months no one in his father's family knew where he spent his leisure hours.

When Henry was not with her, Isabella employed herself in looking after her little garden and the flowers that grew in front of her cottage. The passion-flower peony, dahlia, laburnum, and other plant, so abundant in warm climates, under the tasteful hand of Isabella, lavished their beauty upon this retired spot, and miniature paradise.

Although Isabella had been assured by Henry that she should be free and that he would always consider her as his wife, she nevertheless felt that she ought to be married and acknowledged by him. But this was an impossibility under the State laws, even had the young man been disposed to do what was right in the matter. Related as he was, however, to one of the first families in Virginia, he would not have dared to marry a woman of so low an origin, even had the laws been favorable.

Here, in this secluded grove, unvisited by any other except her lover, Isabella lived for years. She had become the mother of a lovely daughter, which its father named Clotelle. The complexion of the child was still fairer than that of its mother. Indeed, she was not darker than other white children, and as she grew older she more and more resembled her father.

As time passed away, Henry became negligent of Isabella and his child, so much so, that days and even weeks passed without their seeing him, or knowing where he was. Becoming more acquainted with the world, and moving continually in the society of young women of his own station, the young man felt that Isabella was a burden to him, and having as some would say, "outgrown his love," he longed to free himself of the responsibility; yet every time he saw the child, he felt that he owed it his fatherly care.

Henry had now entered into political life, and been elected to a seat in the legislature of his native State; and in his intercourse with his friends had become acquainted with Gertrude Miller, the daughter of a wealthy gentleman living near Richmond. Both Henry and Gertrude were very good-looking, and a mutual attachment sprang up between them.

Instead of finding fault with the unfrequent visits of Henry, Isabella always met him with a smile, and tried to make both him and herself believe that business was the cause of his negligence. When he was with her, she devoted every moment of her time to him, and never failed to speak of the growth and increasing intelligence of Clotelle.

The child had grown so large as to be able to follow its father on his departure out to the road. But the impression made on Henry's feelings by the devoted woman and her child was momentary. His heart had grown hard, and his acts were guided by no fixed principle. Henry and Gertrude had been married nearly two years before Isabella knew anything of the event, and it was merely by accident that she became acquainted with the facts.

One beautiful afternoon, when Isabella and Clotelle were picking wild strawberries some two miles from their home, and near the road-side, they observed a one-horse chaise driving past. The mother turned her face from the carriage not wishing to be seen by strangers, little dreaming that the chaise contained Henry and his wife. The child, however, watched the chaise, and startled her mother by screaming out at the top of her voice, "Papa! papa!" and clapped her little hands for joy. The mother turned in haste to look at the strangers, and her eyes encountered those of Henry's pale and dejected countenance. Gertrude's eyes were on the child. The swiftness with which Henry drove by could not hide from his wife the striking resemblance of the child to himself. The young wife had heard the child exclaim "Papa! papa!" and she immediately saw by the quivering of his lips and the agitation depicted in his countenance, that all was not right.

"Who is that woman? and why did that child call you papa?" she inquired, with a trembling voice.

Henry was silent; he knew not what to say, and without another word passing between them, they drove home.

On reaching her room, Gertrude buried her face in her handkerchief and wept. She loved Henry, and when she had heard from the lips of her companions how their husbands had proved false, she felt that he was an exception, and fervently thanked God that she had been so blessed.

When Gertrude retired to her bed that night, the sad scene of the day followed her. The beauty of Isabella, with her flowing curls, and the look of the child, so much resembling the man whom she so dearly loved, could not be forgotten; and little Clotelle's exclamation of "Papa! Papa" rang in her ears during the whole night.

The return of Henry at twelve o'clock did not increase her happiness. Feeling his guilt, he had absented himself from the house since his return from the ride.

CHAPTER XI
TO-DAY A MISTRESS, TO-MORROW A SLAVE

The night was dark, the rain, descended in torrents from the black and overhanging clouds, and the thunder, accompanied with vivid flashes of lightning, resounded fearfully, as Henry Linwood stepped from his chaise and entered Isabella's cottage.

More than a fortnight had elapsed since the accidental meeting, and Isabella was in doubt as to who the lady was that Henry was with in the carriage. Little, however, did she think that it was his wife. With a smile, Isabella met the young man as he entered her little dwelling. Clotelle had already gone to bed, but her father's voice roused her from her sleep, and she was soon sitting on his knee.

The pale and agitated countenance of Henry betrayed his uneasiness, but Isabella's mild and laughing allusion to the incident of their meeting him on the day of his pleasure-drive, and her saying, "I presume, dear Henry, that the lady was one of your relatives," led him to believe that she was still in ignorance of his marriage.

She was, in fact, ignorant who the lady was who accompanied the man she loved on that eventful day. He, aware of this, now acted more like himself, and passed the thing off as a joke. At heart, however, Isabella felt uneasy, and this uneasiness would at times show itself to the young man. At last, and with a great effort, she said,--

"Now, dear Henry, if I am in the way of your future happiness, say so, and I will release you from any promises that you have made me. I know there is no law by which I can hold you, and if there was, I would not resort to it. You are as dear to me as ever, and my thoughts shall always be devoted to you. It would be a great sacrifice for me to give you up to another, but if it be your desire, as great as the sacrifice is, I will make it. Send me and your child into a Free State if we are in your way."

Again and again Linwood assured her that no woman possessed his love but her. Oh, what falsehood and deceit man can put on when dealing with woman's love!

The unabated storm kept Henry from returning home until after the clock had struck two, and as he drew near his residence he saw his wife standing at the window. Giving his horse in charge of the servant who was waiting, he entered the house, and found his wife in tears. Although he had never satisfied Gertrude as to who the quadroon woman and child were, he had kept her comparatively easy by his close attention to her, and by telling her that she was mistaken in regard to the child's calling him "papa." His absence that night, however, without any apparent cause, had again aroused the jealousy of Gertrude; but Henry told her that he had been caught in the rain while out, which prevented his sooner returning, and she, anxious to believe him, received the story as satisfactory.

Somewhat heated with brandy, and wearied with much loss of sleep, Linwood fell into a sound slumber as soon as he retired. Not so with Gertrude. That faithfulness which has ever distinguished her sex, and the anxiety with which she watched all his movements, kept the wife awake while the husband slept. His sleep, though apparently sound, was nevertheless uneasy. Again and again she heard him pronounce the name of Isabella, and more than once she heard him say, "I am not married; I will never marry while you live." Then he would speak the name of Clotelle and say, "My dear child, how I love you!"

After a sleepless night, Gertrude arose from her couch, resolved that she would reveal the whole matter to her mother. Mrs. Miller was a woman of little or no feeling, proud, peevish, and passionate, thus making everybody miserable that came near her; and when she disliked any one, her hatred knew no bounds. This Gertrude knew; and had she not considered it her duty, she would have kept the secret locked in her own heart.

During the day, Mrs. Linwood visited her mother and told her all that had happened. The mother scolded the daughter for not having informed her sooner, and immediately determined to find out who the woman and child were that Gertrude had met on the day of her ride. Three days were spent by Mrs. Miller in this endeavor, but without success.

Four weeks had elapsed, and the storm of the old lady's temper had somewhat subsided, when, one evening, as she was approaching her daughter's residence, she saw Henry walking, in the direction of where the quadroon was supposed to reside. Feeling satisfied that the young man had not seen her, the old women at once resolved to follow him. Linwood's boots squeaked so loudly that Mrs. Miller had no difficulty in following him without being herself observed.

After a walk of about two miles, the young man turned into a narrow and unfrequented road, and soon entered the cottage occupied by Isabella. It was a fine starlight night, and the moon was just rising when they got to their journey's end. As usual, Isabella met Henry with a smile, and expressed her fears regarding his health.

Hours passed, and still old Mrs. Miller remained near the house, determined to know who lived there. When she undertook to ferret out anything, she bent her whole energies to it. As Michael Angelo, who subjected all things to his pursuit and the idea he had formed of it, painted the crucifixion by the side of a writhing slave and would have broken up the true cross for pencils, so Mrs. Miller would have entered the sepulchre, if she could have done it, in search of an object she wished to find.

The full moon had risen, and was pouring its beams upon surrounding objects as Henry stepped from Isabella's door, and looking at his watch, said,--

"I must go, dear; it is now half-past ten."

Had little Clotelle been awake, she too would have been at the door. As Henry walked to the gate, Isabella followed with her left hand locked in his. Again he looked at his watch, and said, "I must go."

"It is more than a year since you staid all night," murmured Isabella, as he folded her convulsively in his arms, and pressed upon her beautiful lips a parting kiss.

He was nearly out of sight when, with bitter sobs, the quadroon retraced her steps to the door of the cottage. Clotelle had in the mean time awoke, and now inquired of her mother how long her father had been gone. At that instant, a knock was heard at the door, and supposing that it was Henry returning for something he had forgotten, as he frequently did, Isabella flew to let him in. To her amazement, however, a strange woman stood in the door.

"Who are you that comes here at this late hour?" demanded the half-frightened Isabella.

Without making any reply, Mrs. Miller pushed the quadroon aside, and entered the house.

"What do you want here?" again demanded Isabella.

"I am in search of you," thundered the maddened Mrs. Miller; but thinking that her object would be better served by seeming to be kind, she assumed a different tone of voice, and began talking in a pleasing manner.

In this way, she succeeded in finding out the connection existing between Linwood and Isabella, and after getting all she could out of the unsuspecting woman, she informed her that the man she so fondly loved had been married for more than two years. Seized with dizziness, the poor, heart-broken woman fainted and fell upon the floor. How long she remained there she could not tell; but when she returned to consciousness, the strange woman was gone, and her child was standing by her side. When she was so far recovered as to regain her feet, Isabella went to the door, and even into the yard, to see if the old woman was not somewhere about.

As she stood there, the full moon cast its bright rays over her whole person, giving her an angelic appearance and imparting to her flowing hair a still more golden hue. Suddenly another change came over her features, and her full red lips trembled as with suppressed emotion. The muscles around her faultless mouth became convulsed, she gasped for breath, and exclaiming, "Is it possible that man can be so false!" again fainted.

Clotelle stood and bathed her mother's temples with cold water until she once more revived.

Although the laws of Virginia forbid the education of slaves, Agnes had nevertheless employed an old free negro to teach her two daughters to read and write. After being separated from her mother and sister, Isabella turned her attention to the subject of Christianity, and received that consolation from the Bible which is never denied to the children of God. This was now her last hope, for her heart was torn with grief and filled with all the bitterness of disappointment.

The night passed away, but without sleep to poor Isabella. At the dawn of day, she tried to make herself believe that the whole of the past night was a dream, and determined to be satisfied with the explanation which Henry should give on his next visit.

CHAPTER XII
THE MOTHER-IN-LAW.

When Henry returned home, he found his wife seated at the window, awaiting his approach. Secret grief was gnawing at her heart. Her sad, pale cheeks and swollen eyes showed too well that agony, far deeper than her speech portrayed, filled her heart. A dull and death-like silence prevailed on his entrance. His pale face and brow, dishevelled hair, and the feeling that he manifested on finding Gertrude still up, told Henry in plainer words than she could have used that his wife, was aware that her love had never been held sacred by him. The window-blinds were still unclosed, and the full-orbed moon shed her soft refulgence over the unrivalled scene, and gave it a silvery lustre which sweetly harmonized with the silence of the night. The clock's iron tongue, in a neighboring belfry, proclaimed the hour of twelve, as the truant and unfaithful husband seated himself by the side of his devoted and loving wife, and inquired if she was not well.

"I am, dear Henry," replied Gertrude; "but I fear you are not. If well in body, I fear you are not at peace in mind."

"Why?" inquired he.

"Because," she replied, "you are so pale and have such a wild look in your eyes."

Again he protested his innocence, and vowed she was the only woman who had any claim upon his heart. To behold one thus playing upon the feelings of two lovely women is enough to make us feel that evil must at last bring its own punishment.

Henry and Gertrude had scarcely risen from the breakfast-table next morning ere old Mrs. Miller made her appearance. She immediately took her daughter aside, and informed her of her previous night's experience, telling her how she had followed Henry to Isabella's cottage, detailing the interview with the quadroon, and her late return home alone. The old woman urged her daughter to demand that the quadroon and her child be at once sold to the negro speculators and taken out of the State, or that Gertrude herself should separate from Henry.

"Assert your rights, my dear. Let no one share a heart that justly belongs to you," said Mrs. Miller, with her eyes flashing fire. "Don't sleep this night, my child, until that wench has been removed from that cottage; and as for the child, hand that over to me,--I saw at once that it was Henry's."

During these remarks, the old lady was walking up and down the room like a caged lioness. She had learned from Isabella that she had been purchased by Henry, and the innocence of the injured quadroon caused her to acknowledge that he was the father of her child. Few women could have taken such a matter in hand and carried it through with more determination and success than old Mrs. Miller. Completely inured in all the crimes and atrocities connected with the institution of slavery, she was also aware that, to a greater or less extent, the slave women shared with their mistress the affections of their master. This caused her to look with a suspicious eye on every good-looking negro woman that she saw.

While the old woman was thus lecturing her daughter upon her rights and duties, Henry, unaware of what was transpiring, had left the house and gone to his office. As soon as the old woman found that he was gone, she said,--

"I will venture anything that he is on his way to see that wench again. I'll lay my life on it."

The entrance, however, of little Marcus, or Mark, as he was familiarly called, asking for Massa Linwood's blue bag, satisfied her that her son-in-law was at his office. Before the old lady returned home, it was agreed that Gertrude should come to her mother's to tea that evening, and Henry with her, and that Mrs. Miller should there charge the young husband with inconstancy to her daughter, and demand the removal of Isabella.

With this understanding, the old woman retraced her steps to her own dwelling.

Had Mrs. Miller been of a different character and not surrounded by slavery, she could scarcely have been unhappy in such a home as hers. Just at the edge of the city, and sheltered by large poplar-trees was the old homestead in which she resided. There was a splendid orchard in the rear of the house, and the old weather-beaten sweep, with "the moss-covered bucket" at its end, swung majestically over the deep well. The garden was scarcely to be equalled. Its grounds were laid out in excellent taste, and rare exotics in the greenhouse made it still more lovely.

It was a sweet autumn evening, when the air breathed through the fragrant sheaves of grain, and the setting sun, with his golden kisses, burnished the rich clusters of purple grapes, that Henry and Gertrude were seen approaching the house on foot; it was nothing more than a pleasant walk. Oh, how Gertrude's heart beat as she seated herself, on their arrival!

The beautiful parlor, surrounded on all sides with luxury and taste, with the sun creeping through the damask curtains, added a charm to the scene. It was in this room that Gertrude had been introduced to Henry, and the pleasant hours that she had spent there with him rushed unbidden on her memory. It was here that, in former days, her beautiful countenance had made her appearance as fascinating and as lovely as that of Cleopatra's. Her sweet, musical voice might have been heard in every part of the house, occasionally thrilling you with an unexpected touch. How changed the scene! Her pale and wasted features could not be lighted up by any thoughts of the past, and she was sorrowful at heart.

As usual, the servants in the kitchen were in ecstasies at the announcement that "Miss Gerty," as they called their young mistress, was in the house, for they loved her sincerely. Gertrude had saved them from many a flogging, by interceding for them, when her mother was in one of her uncontrollable passions. Dinah, the cook, always expected Miss Gerty to visit the kitchen as soon as she came, and was not a little displeased, on this occasion, at what she considered her young mistress's neglect. Uncle Tony, too, looked regularly for Miss Gerty to visit the green house, and congratulate him on his superiority as a gardener.

When tea was over, Mrs. Miller dismissed the servants from the room, then told her son-in-law what she had witnessed the previous night, and demanded for her daughter that Isabella should be immediately sent out of the State, and to be sure that the thing would be done, she wanted him to give her the power to make such disposition of the woman and child as she should think best. Gertrude was Mrs. Miller's only child, and Henry felt little like displeasing a family upon whose friendship he so much depended, and, no doubt, long wishing to free himself from Isabella, he at once yielded to the demands of his mother-in-law. Mr. Miller was a mere cipher about his premises. If any one came on business connected with the farm, he would invariably say, "Wait tin I see my wife," and the wife's opinion was sure to be law in every case. Bankrupt in character, and debauched in body and mind, with seven mulatto children who claimed him as their father, he was badly prepared to find fault with his son-in-law. It was settled that Mrs. Miller should use her own discretion in removing Isabella from her little cottage, and her future disposition. With this understanding Henry and Gertrude returned home. In the deep recesses of his heart the young man felt that he would like to see his child and its mother once more; but fearing the wrath of his mother-in-law, he did not dare to gratify his inclination. He had not the slightest idea of what would become of them; but he well knew that the old woman would have no mercy on them.

CHAPTER XIII
A HARD-HEARTED WOMAN.

With no one but her dear little Clotelle, Isabella passed her weary hours without partaking of either food or drink, hoping that Henry would soon return, and that the strange meeting with the old woman would be cleared up.

While seated in her neat little bedroom with her fevered face buried in her handkerchief, the child ran in and told its mother that a carriage had stopped in front of the house. With a palpitating heart she arose from her seat and went to the door, hoping that it was Henry; but, to her great consternation, the old lady who had paid her such an unceremonious visit on the evening that she had last seen Henry, stepped out of the carriage, accompanied by the slave-trader, Jennings.

Isabella had seen the trader when he purchased her mother and sister, and immediately recognized him. What could these persons want there? thought she. Without any parleying or word of explanation, the two entered the house, leaving the carriage in charge of a servant.

Clotelle ran to her mother, and clung to her dress as if frightened by the strangers.

"She's a fine-looking wench," said the speculator, as he seated himself, unasked, in the rocking-chair; "yet I don't think she is worth the money you ask for her."

"What do you want here?" inquired Isabella, with a quivering voice.

"None of your insolence to me," bawled out the old woman, at the top of her voice; "if you do, I will give you what you deserve so much, my lady,--a good whipping."

In an agony of grief, pale, trembling, and ready to sink to the floor, Isabella was only sustained by the hope that she would be able to save her child. At last, regaining her self-possession, she ordered them both to leave the house. Feeling herself insulted, the old woman seized the tongs that stood by the fire-place, and raised them to strike the quadroon down; but the slave-trader immediately jumped between the women, exclaiming,--

"I won't buy her, Mrs. Miller, if you injure her."

Poor little Clotelle screamed as she saw the strange woman raise the tongs at her mother. With the exception of old Aunt Nancy, a free colored woman, whom Isabella sometimes employed to work for her, the child had never before seen a strange face in her mother's dwelling. Fearing that Isabella would offer some resistance, Mrs. Miller had ordered the overseer of her own farm to follow her; and, just as Jennings had stepped between the two women, Mull, the negro-driver, walked into the room.

"Seize that impudent hussy," said Mrs. Miller to the overseer, "and tie her up this minute, that I may teach her a lesson she won't forget in a hurry."

As she spoke, the old woman's eyes rolled, her lips quivered, and she looked like a very fury.

"I will have nothing to do with her, if you whip her, Mrs. Miller," said the slave-trader. "Niggers ain't worth half so much in the market with their backs newly scarred," continued he, as the overseer commenced his preparations for executing Mrs. Miller's orders.

Clotelle here took her father's walking-stick, which was lying on the back of the sofa where he had left it, and, raising it, said,--

"If you bad people touch my mother, I will strike you."

They looked at the child with astonishment; and her extreme youth, wonderful beauty, and uncommon courage, seemed for a moment to shake their purpose. The manner and language of this child were alike beyond her years, and under other circumstances would have gained for her the approbation of those present.

"Oh, Henry, Henry!" exclaimed Isabella, wringing her hands.

"You need not call on him, hussy; you will never see him again," said Mrs. Miller.

"What! is he dead?" inquired the heart-stricken woman.

It was then that she forgot her own situation, thinking only of the man she loved. Never having been called to endure any kind of abusive treatment, Isabella was not fitted to sustain herself against the brutality of Mrs. Miller, much less the combined ferociousness of the old woman and the overseer too. Suffice it to say, that instead of whipping Isabella, Mrs. Miller transferred her to the negro-speculator, who took her immediately to his slave-pen. The unfeeling old woman would not permit Isabella to take more than a single change of her clothing, remarking to Jennings,--

"I sold you the wench, you know,--not her clothes."

The injured, friendless, and unprotected Isabella fainted as she saw her child struggling to release herself from the arms of old Mrs. Miller, and as the wretch boxed the poor child's ears.

After leaving directions as to how Isabella's furniture and other effects should be disposed of, Mrs. Miller took Clotelle into her carriage and drove home. There was not even color enough about the child to make it appear that a single drop of African blood flowed through its blue veins.

Considerable sensation was created in the kitchen among the servants when the carriage drove up, and Clotelle entered the house.

"Jes' like Massa Henry fur all de worl," said Dinah, as she caught a glimpse of the child through the window.

"Wondah whose brat dat ar' dat missis bringin' home wid her?" said Jane, as she put the ice in the pitchers for dinner. "I warrant it's some poor white nigger somebody bin givin' her."

The child was white. What should be done to make it look like other negroes, was the question which Mrs. Miller asked herself.

The callous-hearted old woman bit her nether lip, as she viewed that child, standing before her, with her long, dark ringlets clustering over her alabaster brow and neck.

"Take this little nigger and cut her hair close to her head," said the mistress to Jane, as the latter answered the bell.

Clotelle screamed, as she felt the scissors going over her head, and saw those curls that her mother thought so much of falling upon the floor.

A roar of laughter burst from the servants, as Jane led the child through the kitchen, with the hair cut so short that the naked scalp could be plainly seen.

"Gins to look like nigger, now," said Dinah, with her mouth upon a grin.

The mistress smiled, as the shorn child reentered the room; but there was something more needed. The child was white, and that was a great objection. However, she hit upon a plan to remedy this which seemed feasible. The day was excessively warm. Not a single cloud floated over the blue vault of heaven; not a breath of wind seemed moving, and the earth was parched by the broiling sun. Even the bees had stopped humming, and the butterflies had hid themselves under the broad leaves of the burdock. Without a morsel of dinner, the poor child was put in the garden, and set to weeding it, her arms, neck and head completely bare. Unaccustomed to toil, Clotelle wept as she exerted herself in pulling up the weeds. Old Dinah, the cook, was as unfeeling as her mistress, and she was pleased to see the child made to work in the hot sun.

"Dat white nigger 'll soon be black enuff if missis keeps her workin' out dar," she said, as she wiped the perspiration from her sooty brow.

Dinah was the mother of thirteen children, all of whom had been taken from her when young; and this, no doubt, did much to harden her feelings, and make her hate all white persons.

The burning sun poured its rays on the face of the friendless child until she sank down in the corner of the garden, and was actually broiled to sleep.

"Dat little nigger ain't workin' a bit, missus," said Dinah to Mrs. Miller, as the latter entered the kitchen.

"She's lying in the sun seasoning; she will work the better by and by," replied the mistress.

"Dese white niggers always tink dey seff good as white folks," said the cook.

"Yes; but we will teach them better, won't we, Dinah?" rejoined Mrs. Miller.

"Yes, missus," replied Dinah; "I don't like dese merlatter niggers, no how. Dey always want to set dey seff up for sumfin' big." With this remark the old cook gave one of her coarse laughs, and continued: "Missis understands human nature, don't she? Ah! ef she ain't a whole team and de ole gray mare to boot, den Dinah don't know nuffin'."

Of course, the mistress was out of the kitchen before these last marks were made.

It was with the deepest humiliation that Henry learned from one of his own slaves the treatment which his child was receiving at the hands of his relentless mother-in-law.

The scorching sun had the desired effect; for in less than a fortnight, Clotelle could scarcely have been recognized as the same child. Often was she seen to weep, and heard to call on her mother.

Mrs. Miller, when at church on Sabbath, usually, on warm days, took Nancy, one of her servants, in her pew, and this girl had to fan her mistress during service. Unaccustomed to such a soft and pleasant seat, the servant would very soon become sleepy and begin to nod. Sometimes she would go fast asleep, which annoyed the mistress exceedingly. But Mrs. Miller had nimble fingers, and on them sharp nails, and, with an energetic pinch upon the bare arms of the poor girl, she would arouse the daughter of Africa from her pleasant dreams. But there was no one of Mrs. Miller's servants who received as much punishment as old Uncle Tony.

Fond of her greenhouse, and often in the garden, she was ever at the gardener's heels. Uncle Tony was very religious, and, whenever his mistress flogged him, he invariably gave her a religious exhortation. Although unable to read, he, nevertheless, had on his tongue's end portions of Scripture which he could use at any moment. In one end of the greenhouse was Uncle Tony's sleeping room, and those who happened in that vicinity, between nine and ten at night, could hear the old man offering up his thanksgiving to God for his protection during the day. Uncle

Tony, however, took great pride, when he thought that any of the whites were within hearing, to dwell, in his prayer, on his own goodness and the unfitness of others to die. Often was he heard to say, "O Lord, thou knowest that the white folks are not Christians, but the black people are God's own children." But if Tony thought that his old mistress was within the sound of his voice, he launched out into deeper waters.

It was, therefore, on a sweet night, when the bright stars were looking out with a joyous sheen, that Mark and two of the other boys passed the greenhouse, and heard Uncle Tony in his devotions.

"Let's have a little fun," said the mischievous Marcus to his young companions. "I will make Uncle Tony believe that I am old mistress, and he'll give us an extra touch in his prayer." Mark immediately commenced talking in a strain of voice resembling, as well as he could, Mrs. Miller, and at once Tony was heard to say in a loud voice, "O Lord, thou knowest that the white people are not fit to die; but, as for old Tony, whenever the angel of the Lord comes, he's ready." At that moment, Mark tapped lightly on the door. "Who's dar?" thundered old Tony. Mark made no reply. The old man commenced and went through with the same remarks addressed to the Lord, when Mark again knocked at the door. "Who dat dar?" asked Uncle Tony, with a somewhat agitated countenance and trembling voice. Still Mark would not reply. Again Tony took up the thread of his discourse, and said, "O Lord, thou knowest as well as I do that dese white folks are not prepared to die, but here is Old Tony, when de angel of de Lord comes, he's ready to go to heaven." Mark once more knocked at the door. "Who dat dar?" thundered Tony at the top of his voice.

"De angel of de Lord," replied Mark, in a somewhat suppressed and sepulchral voice.

"What de angel of de Lord want here?" inquired Tony, as if much frightened.

"He's come for poor old Tony, to take him out of the world" replied Mark, in the same strange voice.

"Dat nigger ain't here; he die tree weeks ago," responded Tony, in a still more agitated and frightened tone. Mark and his companions made the welkin ring with their shouts at the old man's answer. Uncle Tony hearing them, and finding that he had been imposed upon, opened his door, came out with stick in hand, and said, "Is dat you, Mr. Mark? you imp, if I can get to you I'll larn you how to come here wid your nonsense."

Mark and his companions left the garden, feeling satisfied that Uncle Tony was not as ready to go with "de angel of de Lord" as he would have others believe.

CHAPTER XIV
THE PRISON.

While poor little Clotelle was being kicked about by Mrs. Miller, on account of her relationship to her son-in-law, Isabella was passing lonely hours in the county jail, the place to which Jennings had removed her for safe-keeping, after purchasing her from Mrs. Miller. Incarcerated in one of the iron-barred rooms of that dismal place, those dark, glowing eyes, lofty brow, and graceful form wilted down like a plucked rose under a noonday sun, while deep in her heart's ambrosial cells was the most anguishing distress.

Vulgar curiosity is always in search of its victims, and Jennings' boast that he had such a ladylike and beautiful woman in his possession brought numbers to the prison who begged of the jailer the privilege of seeing the slave-trader's prize. Many who saw her were melted to tears at the pitiful sight, and were struck with admiration at her intelligence; and, when she spoke of her child, they must have been convinced that a mother's sorrow can be conceived by none but a mother's heart. The warbling of birds in the green bowers of bliss, which she occasionally heard, brought no tidings of gladness to her. Their joy fell cold upon her heart, and seemed like bitter mockery. They reminded her of her own cottage, where, with her beloved child, she had spent so many happy days.

The speculator had kept close watch over his valuable piece of property, for fear that it might damage itself. This, however, there was no danger of, for Isabella still hoped and believed that Henry would come to her rescue. She could not bring herself to believe that he would allow her to be sent away without at least seeing her, and the trader did all he could to keep this idea alive in her.

While Isabella, with a weary heart, was passing sleepless nights thinking only of her daughter and Henry, the latter was seeking relief in that insidious enemy of the human race, the intoxicating cup. His wife did all in her power to make his life a pleasant and a happy one, for Gertrude was devotedly attached to him; but a weary heart gets no gladness out of sunshine. The secret remorse that rankled in his bosom caused him to see all the world blood-shot. He had not visited his mother-in-law since the evening he had given her liberty to use her own discretion as to how Isabella and her child should be disposed of. He feared even to go near the house, for he did not wish to see his child. Gertrude felt this every time he declined accompanying her to her mother's. Possessed of a tender and confiding heart, entirely unlike her mother, she sympathized deeply with her husband. She well knew that all young men in the South, to a greater or less extent, became enamored of the slave-women, and she fancied that his case was only one of the many, and if he had now forsaken all others for her she did not wish for him to be punished; but she dared not let her mother know that such were her feelings. Again and again had she noticed the great resemblance between Clotelle and Henry, and she wished the child in better hands than those of her cruel mother.

At last Gertrude determined to mention the matter to her husband. Consequently, the next morning, when they were seated on the back piazza, and the sun was pouring its splendid rays upon everything around, changing the red tints on the lofty hills in the distance into streaks of purest gold, and nature seeming by her smiles to favor the object, she said,--

"What, dear Henry, do you intend to do with Clotelle?"

A paleness that overspread his countenance, the tears that trickled down his cheeks, the deep emotion that was visible in his face, and the trembling of his voice, showed at once that she had touched a tender chord. Without a single word, he buried his face in his handkerchief, and burst into tears.

This made Gertrude still more unhappy, for she feared that he had misunderstood her; and she immediately expressed her regret that she had mentioned the subject. Becoming satisfied from this that his wife sympathized with him in his unhappy situation, Henry told her of the agony that filled his soul, and Gertrude agreed to intercede for him with her mother for the removal of the child to a boarding-school in one of the Free States.

In the afternoon, when Henry returned from his office, his wife met him with tearful eyes, and informed him that her mother was filled with rage at the mere mention of the removal of Clotelle from her premises.

In the mean time, the slave-trader, Jennings, had started for the South with his gang of human cattle, of whom Isabella was one. Most quadroon women who are taken to the South are either sold to gentlemen for their own use or disposed of as house-servants or waiting-maids. Fortunately for Isabella, she was sold, for the latter purpose. Jennings found a purchaser for her in the person of Mr. James French.

Mrs. French was a severe mistress. All who lived with her, though well-dressed, were scantily fed and over-worked. Isabella found her new situation far different from her Virginia cottage-life. She had frequently heard Vicksburg spoken of as a cruel place for slaves, and now she was in a position to test the truthfulness of the assertion.

A few weeks after her arrival, Mrs. French began to show to Isabella that she was anything but a pleasant and agreeable mistress. What social virtues are possible in a society of which injustice is a primary characteristic,--in a society which is divided into two classes, masters and slaves? Every married woman at the South looks upon her husband as unfaithful, and regards every negro woman as a rival.

Isabella had been with her new mistress but a short time when she was ordered to cut off her long and beautiful hair. The negro is naturally fond of dress and outward display. He who has short woolly hair combs and oils it to death; he who has long hair would sooner have his teeth drawn than to part with it. But, however painful it was to Isabella, she was soon seen with her hair cut short, and the sleeves of her dress altered to fit tight to her arms. Even with her hair short and with her ill-looking dress, Isabella was still handsome. Her life had been a secluded one, and though now twenty-eight years of age, her beauty had only assumed a quieter tone. The other servants only laughed at Isabella's misfortune in losing her beautiful hair.

"Miss 'Bell needn't strut so big; she got short nappy har's well's I," said Nell, with a broad grin that showed her teeth.

"She tink she white when she cum here, wid dat long har ob hers," replied Mill.

"Yes," continued Nell, "missus make her take down her wool, so she no put it up to-day."

The fairness of Isabella's complexion was regarded with envy by the servants as well as by the mistress herself. This is one of the hard features of slavery. To-day a woman is mistress of her own cottage; to-morrow she is sold to one who aims to make her life as intolerable as possible. And let it be remembered that the house-servant has the best situation a slave can occupy.

But the degradation and harsh treatment Isabella experienced in her new home was nothing compared to the grief she underwent at being separated from her dear child. Taken from her with scarcely a moment's warning, she knew not what had become of her.

This deep and heartfelt grief of Isabella was soon perceived by her owners, and fearing that her refusal to take proper food would cause her death, they resolved to sell her. Mr. French found no difficulty in securing a purchaser for the quadroon woman, for such are usually the most marketable kind of property. Isabella was sold at private sale to a young man for a housekeeper; but even he had missed his aim.

Mr. Gordon, the new master, was a man of pleasure. He was the owner of a large sugar plantation, which he had left under the charge of an overseer, and was now giving himself up to the pleasures of a city life. At first Mr. Gordon sought to win Isabella's favor by flattery and presents, knowing that whatever he gave her he could take from her again. The poor innocent creature dreaded every moment lest the scene should change. At every interview with Gordon she stoutly maintained that she had left a husband in Virginia, and could never think of taking another. In this she considered that she was truthful, for she had ever regarded Henry as her husband. The gold watch and chain and other glittering presents which Gordon gave to her were all kept unused.

In the same house with Isabella was a man-servant who had from time to time hired himself from his master. His name was William. He could feel for Isabella, for he, like her, had been separated from near and dear relatives, and he often tried to console the poor woman. One day Isabella observed to him that her hair was grow-ing out again.

"Yes," replied William; "you look a good deal like a man with your short hair."

"Oh," rejoined she, "I have often been told that I would make a better looking man than woman, and if I had the money I might avail myself of it to bid farewell to this place."

In a moment afterwards, Isabella feared that she had said too much, and laughingly observed, "I am always talking some nonsense; you must not heed me."

William was a tall, full-blooded African, whose countenance beamed with intelligence. Being a mechanic, he had by industry earned more money than he had paid to his owner for his time, and this he had laid aside, with the hope that he might some day get enough to purchase his freedom. He had in his chest about a hundred and fifty dollars. His was a heart that felt for others, and he had again and again wiped the tears from his eyes while listening to Isabella's story.

"If she can get free with a little money, why not give her what I have?" thought he, and then resolved to do it.

An hour after, he entered the quadroon's room, and, laying the money in her lap, said,--

"There, Miss Isabella, you said just now that if you had the means you would leave this place. There is money enough to take you to England, where you will be free. You are much fairer than many of the white women of the South, and can easily pass for a free white woman."

At first Isabella thought it was a plan by which the negro wished to try her fidelity to her owner; but she was soon convinced, by his earnest manner and the deep feeling he manifested, that he was entirely sincere.

"I will take the money," said she, "only on one condition, and that is that I effect your escape, as well as my own."

"How can that be done?" he inquired, eagerly.

"I will assume the disguise of a gentleman, and you that of a servant, and we will thus take passage in a steamer to Cincinnati, and from thence to Canada."

With full confidence in Isabella's judgment, William consented at once to the proposition. The clothes were purchased; everything was arranged, and the next night, while Mr. Gordon was on one of his sprees, Isabella, under the assumed name of Mr. Smith, with William in attendance as a servant, took passage for Cincinnati in the steamer Heroine.

With a pair of green glasses over her eyes, in addition to her other disguise, Isabella made quite a gentlemanly appearance. To avoid conversation, however, she kept closely to her state-room, under the plea of illness.

Meanwhile, William was playing his part well with the servants. He was loudly talking of his master's wealth, and nothing on the boat appeared so good as in his master's fine mansion.

"I don't like dese steamboats, no how," said he; "I hope when massa goes on anoder journey, he take de carriage and de hosses."

After a nine-days' passage, the Heroine landed at Cincinnati, and Mr. Smith and his servant walked on shore.

"William, you are now a free man, and can go on to Canada," said Isabella; "I shall go to Virginia, in search of my daughter."

This sudden announcement fell heavily upon William's ears, and with tears he besought her not to jeopardize her liberty in such a manner; but Isabella had made up her mind to rescue her child if possible.

Taking a boat for Wheeling, Isabella was soon on her way to her native State. Several months had elapsed since she left Richmond, and all her thoughts were centred on the fate of her dear Clotelle. It was with a palpitating heart that this injured woman entered the stage-coach at Wheeling and set out for Richmond.

CHAPTER XV
THE ARREST.

It was late in the evening when the coach arrived at Richmond, and Isabella once more alighted in her native city. She had intended to seek lodgings somewhere in the outskirts of the town, but the lateness of the hour compelled her to stop at one of the principal hotels for the night. She had scarcely entered the inn before she recognized among the numerous black servants one to whom she was well known, and her only hope was that her disguise would keep her from being discovered. The imperturbable calm and entire forgetfulness of self which induced Isabella to visit a place from which she could scarcely hope to escape, to attempt the rescue of a beloved child, demonstrate that over-willingness of woman to carry out the promptings of the finer feelings of the heart. True to woman's nature, she had risked her own liberty for another's. She remained in the hotel during the night, and the next morning, under the plea of illness, took her breakfast alone.

That day the fugitive slave paid a visit to the suburbs of the town, and once more beheld the cottage in which she had spent so many happy hours. It was winter, and the clematis and passion-flower were not there; but there were the same walks her feet had so often pressed, and the same trees which had so often shaded her as she passed through the garden at the back of the house. Old remembrances rushed upon her memory and caused her to shed tears freely. Isabella was now in her native town, and near her daughter; but how could she communicate with her? how could she see her? To have made herself known would have been a suicidal act; betrayal would have followed, and she arrested. Three days passed away, and still she remained in the hotel at which she had first put up, and yet she got no tidings of her child.

Unfortunately for Isabella, a disturbance had just broken out among the slave population in the State of Virginia, and all strangers were treated with suspicion.

The insurrection to which we now refer was headed by a full-blooded negro, who had been born and brought up a slave. He had heard the crack of the driver's whip, and seen the warm blood streaming from the negro's body. He had witnessed the separation of parents from children, and was made aware, by too many proofs, that the slave could expect no justice from the hands of the slave-owner. The name of this man was Nat Turner. He was a preacher amongst the negroes, distinguished for his eloquence, respected by the whites, loved and venerated by the negroes. On the discovery of the plan for the outbreak, Turner fled to the swamps, followed by those who had joined in the insurrection.

Here the revolted negroes numbered some hundreds, and for a time bade defiance to their oppressors. The Dismal Swamps cover many thousand acres of wild land, and a dense forest, with wild animals and insects such as are unknown in any other part of Virginia. Here runaway negroes usually seek a hiding-place, and some have been known to reside here for years. The revolters were joined by one of these. He was a large, tall, full-blooded negro, with a stern and savage countenance; the marks on his face showed that he was from one of the barbarous tribes in Africa, and claimed that country as his native land. His only covering was a girdle around his loins, made of skins of wild beasts which he had killed. His only token of authority among those that he led was a pair of epaulettes, made of the tail of a fox, and tied to his shoulder by a cord. Brought from the coast of Africa, when only fifteen years of age, to the island of Cuba, he was smuggled from thence into Virginia. He had been two years in the swamps, and considered it his future home. He had met a negro woman, who was also a runaway, and, after the fashion of his native land, had gone through the process of oiling her, as the marriage ceremony. They had built a cave on a rising mound in the swamp, and this was their home. This man's name was Picquilo. His only weapon was a sword made from a scythe which he had stolen from a neighboring plantation. His dress, his character, his manners, and his mode of fighting were all in keeping with the early training he had received in the land of his birth. He moved about with the activity of a cat, and neither the thickness of the trees nor the depth of the water could stop him. His was a bold, turbulent spirit; and, from motives of revenge, he imbrued his hands in the blood of all the whites he could meet. Hunger, thirst, and loss of sleep, he seemed made to endure, as if by peculiarity of constitution. His air was fierce, his step oblique, his look sanguinary.

Such was the character of one of the negroes in the Southampton Insurrection. All negroes were arrested who were found beyond their master's threshold, and all white strangers were looked upon with suspicion.

Such was the position in which Isabella found affairs when she returned to Virginia in search of her child. Had not the slave-owners been watchful of strangers, owing to the outbreak, the fugitive could not have escaped the vigilance of the police; for advertisements announcing her escape, and offering a large reward for her arrest, had been received in the city previous to her arrival, and officers were therefore on the lookout for her.

It was on the third day after her arrival in Richmond, as the quadroon was seated in her room at the hotel, still in the disguise of a gentleman, that two of the city officers entered the apartment and informed her that they were authorized to examine all strangers, to assure the authorities that they were not in league with the revolted negroes.

With trembling heart the fugitive handed the key of her trunk to the officers. To their surprise they found nothing but female apparel in the trunk, which raised their curiosity, and caused a further investigation that resulted in the arrest of Isabella as a fugitive slave. She was immediately conveyed to prison, there to await the orders of her master.

For many days, uncheered by the voice of kindness, alone, hopeless, desolate, she waited for the time to arrive when the chains should be placed on her limbs, and she returned to her inhuman and unfeeling owner.

The arrest of the fugitive was announced in all the newspapers, but created little or no sensation. The inhabitants were too much engaged in putting down the revolt among the slaves; and, although all the odds were against the insurgents, the whites found it no easy matter, with all their caution. Every day brought news of fresh outbreaks. Without scruple and without pity, the whites massacred all blacks found beyond the limits of their owners' plantations. The negroes, in return, set fire to houses, and put to death those who attempted to escape from the flames. Thus carnage was added to carnage, and the blood of the whites flowed to avenge the blood of the blacks.

These were the ravages of slavery. No graves were dug for the negroes, but their bodies became food for dogs and vultures; and their bones, partly calcined by the sun, remained scattered about, as if to mark the mournful fury of servitude and lust of power. When the slaves were subdued, except a few in the swamps, blood-hounds were employed to hunt out the remaining revolters.

CHAPTER XVI
DEATH IS FREEDOM.

On receiving intelligence of the arrest of Isabella, Mr. Gordon authorized the sheriff to sell her to the highest bidder. She was, therefore, sold; the purchaser being the noted negro-trader, Hope H. Slater, who at once placed her in prison. Here the fugitive saw none but slaves like herself, brought in and taken out to be placed in ships, and sent away to some part of the country to which she herself would soon be compelled to go. She had seen or heard nothing of her daughter while in Richmond, and all hopes of seeing her had now fled.

At the dusk of the evening previous to the day when she was to be sent off, as the old prison was being closed for the night, Isabella suddenly darted past the keeper, and ran for her life. It was not a great distance from the prison to the long bridge which passes from the lower part of the city across the Potomac to the extensive forests and woodlands of the celebrated Arlington Heights, then occupied by that distinguished relative and descendant of the immortal Washington, Mr.

Geo. W. Custis. Thither the poor fugitive directed her flight. So unexpected was her escape that she had gained several rods the start before the keeper had secured the other prisoners, and rallied his assistants to aid in the pursuit. It was at an hour, and in a part of the city where horses could not easily be obtained for the chase; no bloodhounds were at hand to run down the flying woman, and for once it seemed as if there was to be a fair trial of speed and endurance between the slave and the slave-catchers.

The keeper and his force raised the hue-and-cry on her path as they followed close behind; but so rapid was the flight along the wide avenue that the astonished citizens, as they poured forth from their dwellings to learn the cause of alarm, were only able to comprehend the nature of the case in time to fall in with the motley throng in pursuit, or raise an anxious prayer to heaven as they refused to join in the chase (as many a one did that night) that the panting fugitive might escape, and the merciless soul-dealer for once be disappointed of his prey. And now, with the speed of an arrow, having passed the avenue, with the distance between her and her pursuers constantly increasing, this poor, hunted female gained the "Long Bridge," as it is called, where interruption seemed improbable. Already her heart began to beat high with the hope of success. She had only to pass three-quarters of a mile across the bridge, when she could bury herself in a vast forest, just at the time when the curtain of night would close around her, and protect her from the pursuit of her enemies.

But God, by his providence, had otherwise determined. He had ordained that an appalling tragedy should be enacted that night within plain sight of the President's house, and the Capitol of the Union, which would be an evidence wherever it should be known of the unconquerable love of liberty which the human heart may inherit, as well as a fresh admonition to the slave-dealer of the cruelty and enormity of his crimes.

Just as the pursuers passed the high draw, soon after entering upon the bridge, they beheld three men slowly approaching from the Virginia side. They immediately called to them to arrest the fugitive, proclaiming her a runaway slave. True to their Virginia instincts, as she came near, they formed a line across the narrow bridge to intercept her. Seeing that escape was impossible in that quarter, she stopped suddenly, and turned upon her pursuers.

On came the profane and ribald crew faster than ever, already exulting in her capture, and threatening punishment for her flight. For a moment she looked wildly and anxiously around to see if there was no hope of escape. On either hand, far down below, rolled the deep, foaming waters of the Potomac, and before and behind were the rapidly approaching steps and noisy voices of her pursuers. Seeing how vain would be any further effort to escape, her resolution was instantly taken. She clasped her hands convulsively together, raised her tearful and imploring eyes toward heaven, and begged for the mercy and compassion there which was unjustly denied her on earth; then, exclaiming, "Henry, Clotelle, I die for thee!" with a single bound, vaulted over, the railing of the bridge, and sank forever beneath the angry and foaming waters of the river!

Such was the life, and such the death, of a woman whose virtues and goodness of heart would have done honor to one in a higher station of life, and who, had she been born in any other land but that of slavery, would have been respected and beloved. What would have been her feelings if she could have known that the child for whose rescue she had sacrificed herself would one day be free, honored, and loved in another land?

CHAPTER XVII
CLOTELLE.

The curtain rises seven years after the death of Isabella. During that interval, Henry, finding that nothing could induce his mother-in-law to relinquish her hold on poor little Clotelle, and not liking to contend with one on whom a future fortune depended, gradually lost all interest in the child, and left her to her fate.

Although Mrs. Miller treated Clotelle with a degree of harshness scarcely equalled, when applied to one so tender in years, still the child grew every day more beautiful, and her hair, though kept closely cut, seemed to have improved in its soft, silk-like appearance. Now twelve years of age, and more than usually well-developed, her harsh old mistress began to view her with a jealous eye.

Henry and Gertrude had just returned from Washington, where the husband had been on his duties as a member of Congress, and where he had remained during the preceding three years without returning home. It was on a beautiful evening, just at twilight, while seated at his parlor window, that Henry saw a young woman pass by and go into the kitchen. Not aware of ever having seen the person before, he made an errand into the cook's department to see who the girl was. He, however, met her in the hall, as she was about going out.

"Whom did you wish to see?" he inquired.

"Miss Gertrude," was the reply.

"What did you want to see her for?" he again asked.

"My mistress told me to give her and Master Henry her compliments, and ask them to come over and spend the evening."

"Who is your mistress?" he eagerly inquired.

"Mrs. Miller, sir," responded the girl.

"And what's your name?" asked Henry, with a trembling voice.

"Clotelle, sir," was the reply.

The astonished father stood completely amazed, looking at the now womanly form of her who, in his happier days, he had taken on his knee with so much fondness and alacrity. It was then that he saw his own and Isabella's features combined in the beautiful face that he was then beholding. It was then that he was carried back to the days when with a woman's devotion, poor Isabella hung about his neck and told him how lonely were the hours in his absence. He could stand it no longer. Tears rushed to his eyes, and turning upon his heel, he went back to his own room. It was then that Isabella was revenged; and she no doubt looked smilingly down from her home in the spirit-land on the scene below.

On Gertrude's return from her shopping tour, she found Henry in a melancholy mood, and soon learned its cause. As Gertrude had borne him no children, it was but natural, that he should now feel his love centering in Clotelle, and he now intimated to his wife his determination to remove his daughter from the hands of his mother-in-law.

When this news reached Mrs. Miller, through her daughter, she became furious with rage, and calling Clotelle into her room, stripped her shoulders bare and flogged her in the presence of Gertrude.

It was nearly a week after the poor girl had been so severely whipped and for no cause whatever, that her father learned of the circumstance through one of the servants. With a degree of boldness unusual for him, he immediately went to his mother-in-law and demanded his child. But it was too late,--she was gone. To what place she had been sent no one could tell, and Mrs. Miller refused to give any information whatever relative to the girl.

It was then that Linwood felt deepest the evil of the institution under which he was living; for he knew that his daughter would be exposed to all the vices prevalent in that part of the country where marriage is not recognized in connection with that class.

CHAPTER XVIII
A SLAVE-HUNTING PARSON.

It was a delightful evening after a cloudless day, with the setting sun reflecting his golden rays on the surrounding hills which were covered with a beautiful greensward, and the luxuriant verdure that forms the constant garb of the tropics, that the steamer Columbia ran into the dock at Natchez, and began unloading the cargo, taking in passengers and making ready to proceed on her voyage to New Orleans. The plank connecting the boat with the shore had scarcely been secured in its place, when a good-looking man about fifty years of age, with a white neck-tie, and a pair of gold-rimmed glasses on, was seen hurrying on board the vessel. Just at that moment could be seen a stout man with his face pitted with the small-pox, making his way up to the above-mentioned gentleman.

"How do you do, my dear sir? this is Mr. Wilson, I believe," said the short man, at the same time taking from his mouth a large chew of tobacco, and throwing it down on the ship's deck.

"You have the advantage of me, sir," replied the tall man.

"Why, don't you know me? My name is Jennings; I sold you a splendid negro woman some years ago."

"Yes, yes," answered the Natchez man. "I remember you now, for the woman died in a few months, and I never got the worth of my money out of her."

"I could not help that," returned the slave-trader; "she was as sound as a roach when I sold her to you."

"Oh, yes," replied the parson, "I know she was; but now I want a young girl, fit for house use,--one that will do to wait on a lady."

"I am your man," said Jennings, "just follow me," continued he, "and I will show you the fairest little critter you ever saw." And the two passed to the stern of the boat to where the trader had between fifty and sixty slaves, the greater portion being women.

"There," said Jennings, as a beautiful young woman shrunk back with modesty. "There, sir, is the very gal that was made for you. If she had been made to your order, she could not have suited you better."

"Indeed, sir, is not that young woman white?" inquired the parson.

"Oh, no, sir; she is no whiter than you see!"

"But is she a slave?" asked the preacher.

"Yes," said the trader, "I bought her in Richmond, and she comes from an excellent family. She was raised by Squire Miller, and her mistress was one of the most pious ladies in that city, I may say; she was the salt of the earth, as the ministers say."

"But she resembles in some respect Agnes, the woman I bought from you," said Mr. Wilson. As he said the name of Agnes, the young woman started as if she had been struck. Her pulse seemed to quicken, but her face alternately flushed and turned pale, and tears trembled upon her eyelids. It was a name she had heard her mother mention, and it brought to her memory those days,--those happy days, when she was so loved and caressed. This young woman was Clotelle, the granddaughter of Agnes. The preacher, on learning the fact, purchased her, and took her home, feeling that his daughter Georgiana would prize her very highly. Clotelle found in Georgiana more a sister than a mistress, who, unknown to her father, taught the slave-girl how to read, and did much toward improving and refining Clotelle's manners, for her own sake. Like her mother fond of flowers, the "Virginia Maid," as she was sometimes called, spent many of her leisure hours in the garden. Beside the flowers which sprang up from the fertility of soil unplanted and unattended, there was the heliotrope, sweet-pea, and cup-rose, transplanted from the island of Cuba. In her new home Clotelle found herself saluted on all sides by the fragrance of the magnolia. When she went with her young mistress to the Poplar Farm, as she sometimes did, nature's wild luxuriance greeted her, wherever she cast her eyes.

The rustling citron, lime, and orange, shady mango with its fruits of gold, and the palmetto's umbrageous beauty, all welcomed the child of sorrow. When at the farm, Huckelby, the overseer, kept his eye on Clotelle if within sight of her, for he knew she was a slave, and no doubt hoped that she might some day fall into his hands. But she shrank from his looks as she would have done from the charm of the rattlesnake. The negro-driver always tried to insinuate himself into the good opinion of Georgiana and the company that she brought. Knowing that Miss Wilson at heart hated slavery, he was ever trying to show that the slaves under his charge were happy and contented. One day, when Georgiana and some of her Connecticut friends were there, the overseer called all the slaves up to the "great house," and set some of the young ones to dancing. After awhile whiskey was brought in and a dram given to each slave, in return for which they were expected to give a toast, or sing a short piece of his own composition; when it came to Jack's turn he said,--

"The big bee flies high, the little bee makes the honey: the black folks make the cotton, and the white folks gets the money."

Of course, the overseer was not at all elated with the sentiment contained in Jack's toast. Mr. Wilson had lately purchased a young man to assist about the house and to act as coachman. This slave, whose name was Jerome, was of pure African origin, was perfectly black, very fine-looking, tall, slim, and erect as any one could possibly be. His features were not bad, lips thin, nose prominent, hands and feet small. His brilliant black eyes lighted up his whole countenance. His hair which was nearly straight, hung in curls upon his lofty brow. George Combe or Fowler would have selected his head for a model. He was brave and daring, strong in person, fiery in spirit, yet kind and true in his affections, earnest in his doctrines. Clotelle had been at the parson's but a few weeks when it was observed that a mutual feeling had grown up between her and Jerome. As time rolled on, they became more and more attached to each other. After satisfying herself that these two really loved, Georgiana advised their marriage. But Jerome contemplated his escape at some future day, and therefore feared that if married it might militate against it. He hoped, also, to be able to get Clotelle away too, and it was this hope that kept him from trying to escape by himself. Dante did not more love his Beatrice, Swift his Stella, Waller his Saccharissa, Goldsmith his Jessamy bride, or Bums his Mary, than did Jerome his Clotelle. Unknown to her father, Miss Wilson could permit these two slaves to enjoy more privileges than any of the other servants. The young mistress taught Clotelle, and the latter imparted her instructions to her lover, until both could read so as to be well understood. Jerome felt his superiority, and always declared that no master should ever flog him. Aware of his high spirit and determination, Clotelle was in constant fear lest some difficulty might arise between her lover and his master.

One day Mr. Wilson, being somewhat out of temper and irritated at what he was pleased to call Jerome's insolence, ordered him to follow him to the barn to be flogged. The young slave obeyed his master, but those who saw him at the moment felt that he would not submit to be whipped.

"No, sir," replied Jerome, as his master told him to take off his coat. "I will serve you, Master Wilson, I will labor for you day and night, if you demand it, but I will not be whipped."

This was too much for a white man to stand from a negro, and the preacher seized his slave by the throat, intending to choke him. But for once he found his match. Jerome knocked him down, and then escaped through the back-yard to the street, and from thence to the woods.

Recovering somewhat from the effect of his fall, the parson regained his feet and started in pursuit of the fugitive. Finding, however, that the slave was beyond his reach, he at once resolved to put the dogs on his track. Tabor, the negro-catcher, was sent for, and in less than an hour, eight or ten men, including the parson, were in the woods with hounds, trying the trails. These dogs will attack a negro at their master's bidding; and cling to him as the bull-dog will cling to a beast. Many are the speculations as to whether the negro will be secured alive or dead, when these dogs once get on his track. Whenever there is to be a negro hunt, there is no lack of participants. Many go to enjoy the fun which it is said they derive from these scenes.

The company had been in the woods but a short time ere they got on the track of two fugitives, one of whom was Jerome. The slaves immediately bent their steps toward the swamp, with the hope that the dogs, when put upon their scent would be unable to follow them through the water.

The slaves then took a straight course for the Baton Rouge and Bayou Sara road, about four miles distant. Nearer and nearer the whimpering pack pressed on;

their delusion begins to dispel. All at once the truth flashes upon the minds of the fugitives like a glare of light,--'tis Tabor with his dogs!

The scent becomes warmer and warmer, and what was at first an irregular cry now deepens into one ceaseless roar, as the relentless pack presses on after its human prey.

They at last reach the river, and in the negroes plunge, followed by the catch-dog. Jerome is caught and is once more in the hands of his master, while the other poor fellow finds a watery grave. They return, and the preacher sends his slave to jail.

CHAPTER XIX
THE TRUE HEROINE.

In vain did Georgiana try to console Clotelle, when the latter heard, through one of the other slaves, that Mr. Wilson had started with the dogs in pursuit of Jerome. The poor girl well knew that he would be caught, and that severe punishment, if not death, would be the result of his capture. It was therefore with a heart filled with the deepest grief that the slave-girl heard the footsteps of her master on his return from the chase. The dogged and stern manner of the preacher forbade even his daughter inquiring as to the success of his pursuit. Georgiana secretly hoped that the fugitive had not been caught; she wished it for the sake of the slave, and more especially for her maid-servant, whom she regarded more as a companion than a menial. But the news of the capture of Jerome soon spread through the parson's household, and found its way to the ears of the weeping and heart-stricken Clotelle.

The reverend gentleman had not been home more than an hour ere come of his parishioners called to know if they should not take the negro from the prison and execute Lynch law upon him.

"No negro should be permitted to live after striking a white man; let us take him and hang him at once," remarked an elderly-looking man, whose gray hairs thinly covered the crown of his head.

"I think the deacon is right," said another of the company; "if our slaves are allowed to set the will of their masters at defiance, there will be no getting along with them,--an insurrection will be the next thing we hear of."

"No, no," said the preacher; "I am willing to let the law take its course, as it provides for the punishment of a slave with death if he strikes his master. We had better let the court decide the question. Moreover, as a Christian and God-fearing people, we ought to submit to the dictates of justice. Should we take this man's life by force, an All-wise Providence would hold us responsible for the act."

The company then quietly withdrew, showing that the preacher had some influence with his people.

"This" said Mr. Wilson, when left alone with his daughter,--"this, my dear Georgiana, is the result of your kindness to the negroes. You have spoiled every one about the house. I can't whip one of them, without being in danger of having my life taken."

"I am sure, papa," replied the young lady,--"I am sure I never did any thing intentionally to induce any of the servants to disobey your orders."

"No, my dear," said Mr. Wilson, "but you are too kind to them. Now, there is Clotelle,--that girl is completely spoiled. She walks about the house with as dignified an air as if she was mistress of the premises. By and by you will be sorry for this foolishness of yours."

"But," answered Georgiana, "Clotelle has a superior mind, and God intended her to hold a higher position in life than that of a servant."

"Yes, my dear, and it was your letting her know that she was intended for a better station in society that is spoiling her. Always keep a negro in ignorance of what you conceive to be his abilities," returned the parson.

It was late on the Saturday afternoon, following the capture of Jerome that, while Mr. Wilson was seated in his study preparing his sermon for the next day, Georgiana entered the room and asked in an excited tone if it were true that Jerome was to be hanged on the following Thursday.

The minister informed her that such was the decision of the court.

"Then," said she, "Clotelle will die of grief."

"What business has she to die of grief?" returned the father, his eyes at the moment flashing fire.

"She has neither eaten nor slept since he was captured," replied Georgians;

"and I am certain that she will not live through this."

"I cannot be disturbed now," said the parson; "I must get my sermon ready for to-morrow. I expect to have some strangers to preach to, and must, therefore, prepare a sermon that will do me credit."

While the man of God spoke, he seemed to say to himself,--

"With devotion's visage, and pious actions, We do sugar over the devil himself."

Georgiana did all in her power to soothe the feelings of Clotelle, and to induce her to put her trust in God. Unknown to her father, she allowed the poor girl to go every evening to the jail to see Jerome, and during these visits, despite her own grief, Clotelle would try to comfort her lover with the hope that justice would be meted out to him in the spirit-land.

Thus the time passed on, and the day was fast approaching when the slave was to die. Having heard that some secret meeting had been held by the negroes, previous to the attempt of Mr. Wilson to flog his slave, it occurred to a magistrate that Jerome might know something of the intended revolt. He accordingly visited the prison to see if he could learn anything from him, but all to no purpose. Having given up all hopes of escape, Jerome had resolved to die like a brave man. When questioned as to whether he knew anything of a conspiracy among the slaves against their masters, he replied,--

"Do you suppose that I would tell you if I did?"

"But if you know anything," remarked the magistrate, "and will tell us, you may possibly have your life spared."

"Life," answered the doomed man, "is worth nought to a slave. What right has a slave to himself, his wife, or his children? We are kept in heathenish darkness, by laws especially enacted to make our instruction a criminal offence; and our bones, sinews, blood, and nerves are exposed in the market for sale.

"My liberty is of as much consequence to me as Mr. Wilson's is to him. I am as sensitive to feeling as he. If I mistake not, the day will come when the negro will learn that he can get his freedom by fighting for it; and should that time arrive, the whites will be sorry that they have hated us so shamefully. I am free to say that, could I live my life over again, I would use all the energies which God has given me to get up an insurrection."

Every one present seemed startled and amazed at the intelligence with which this descendant of Africa spoke.

"He's a very dangerous man," remarked one.

"Yes," said another, "he got some book-learning somewhere, and that has spoiled him."

An effort was then made to learn from Jerome where he had learned to read, but the black refused to give any information on the subject.

The sun was just going down behind the trees as Clotelle entered the prison to see Jerome for the last time. He was to die on the next day Her face was bent upon her hands, and the gushing tears were forcing their way through her fingers. With beating heart and trembling hands, evincing the deepest emotion, she threw her arms around her lover's neck and embraced him. But, prompted by her heart's unchanging love, she had in her own mind a plan by which she hoped to effect the escape of him to whom she had pledged her heart and hand. While the overcharged clouds which had hung over the city during the day broke, and the rain fell in torrents, amid the most terrific thunder and lightning, Clotelle revealed to Jerome her plan for his escape.

"Dress yourself in my clothes," said she, "and you can easily pass the jailer."

This Jerome at first declined doing. He did not wish to place a confiding girl in a position where, in all probability, she would have to suffer; but being assured by the young girl that her life would not be in danger, he resolved to make the attempt. Clotelle being very tall, it was not probable that the jailer would discover any difference in them.

At this moment, she took from her pocket a bunch of keys and unfastened the padlock, and freed him from the floor.

"Come, girl, it is time for you to go," said the jailer, as Jerome was holding the almost fainting girl by the hand.

Being already attired in Clotelle's clothes, the disguised man embraced the weeping girl, put his handkerchief to his face, and passed out of the jail, without the keeper's knowing that his prisoner was escaping in a disguise and under cover of the night.

CHAPTER XX
THE HERO OF MANY ADVENTURES.

Jerome had scarcely passed the prison-gates, ere he reproached himself for having taken such a step. There seemed to him no hope of escape out of the State, and what was a few hours or days at most, of life to him, when, by obtaining it, another had been sacrificed. He was on the eve of returning, when he thought of the last words uttered by Clotelle. "Be brave and determined, and you will still be free." The words sounded like a charm in his ears and he went boldly forward.

Clotelle had provided a suit of men's clothes and had placed them where her lover could get them, if he should succeed in getting out.

Returning to Mr. Wilson's barn, the fugitive changed his apparel, and again retraced his steps into the street. To reach the Free States by travelling by night and lying by during the day, from a State so far south as Mississippi, no one would think for a moment of attempting to escape. To remain in the city would be a suicidal step. The deep sound of the escape of steam from a boat, which was at that moment ascending the river, broke upon the ears of the slave. "If that boat is going up the river," said he, "why not I conceal myself on board, and try to escape?" He went at once to the steamboat landing, where the boat was just coming in. "Bound for Louisville," said the captain, to one who was making inquiries. As the passengers were rushing on board, Jerome followed them, and proceeding to where some of the hands were stowing away bales of goods, he took hold and aided them.

"Jump down into the hold, there, and help the men," said the mate to the fugitive, supposing that, like many persons, he was working his way up the river. Once in the hull among the boxes, the slave concealed himself. Weary hours, and at last days, passed without either water or food with the hidden slave. More than once did he resolve to let his case be known; but the knowledge that he would be sent back to Natchez kept him from doing so. At last, with lips parched and fevered to a crisp, the poor man crawled out into the freight-room, and began wandering about. The hatches were on, and the room dark. There happened to be on board a wedding party, and, a box, containing some of the bridal cake, with several bottles of port wine, was near Jerome. He found the box, opened it, and helped himself. In eight days, the boat tied up at the wharf at the place of her destination. It was late at night; the boat's crew, with the single exception of the man on watch, were on shore. The hatches were off, and the fugitive quietly made his way on deck and jumped on shore. The man saw the fugitive, but too late to seize him.

Still in a Slave State, Jerome was at a loss to know how he should proceed. He had with him a few dollars, enough to pay his way to Canada, if he could find a conveyance. The fugitive procured such food as he wanted from one of the many eating-houses, and then, following the direction of the North Star, he passed out of the city, and took the road leading to Covington. Keeping near the Ohio River, Jerome soon found an opportunity to cross over into the State of Indiana. But liberty was a mere name in the latter State, and the fugitive learned, from some colored persons that he met, that it was not safe to travel by daylight. While making his way one night, with nothing to cheer him but the prospect of freedom in the future, he was pounced upon by three men who were lying in wait for another fugitive, an advertisement of whom they had received through the mail. In vain did Jerome tell them that he was not a slave. True, they had not caught the man they expected; but, if they could make this slave tell from what place he had escaped, they knew that a good price would be paid them for the negro's arrest.

Tortured by the slave-catchers, to make him reveal the name of his master and the place from whence he had escaped, Jerome gave them a fictitious name in Virginia, and said that his master would give a large reward, and manifested a willingness to return to his "old boss." By this misrepresentation, the fugitive, hoped to have another chance of getting away. Allured with the prospect of a large sum of the needful, the slave-catchers started back with their victim. Stopping on the second night at an inn, on the banks of the Ohio River, the kidnappers, in lieu of a suitable place in which to confine their prize during the night, chained him to the bed-post of their sleeping-chamber. The white men were late in retiring to rest, after an evening spent in drinking. At dead of night, when all was still, the slave arose from the floor, upon which he had been lying, looked around and saw that Morpheus had possession of his captors. For once, thought he, the brandy bottle has done a noble work. With palpitating heart and trembling limbs, he viewed his position. The door was fast, but the warm weather had compelled them to leave the window open. If he could but get his chains off, he might escape through the window to the piazza. The sleepers' clothes hung upon chairs by the bedside. The slave thought of the padlock-key, examined the pockets, and found it. The chains were soon off, and the negro stealthily making his way to the window. He stopped, and said to himself, "These men are villains; they are enemies to all who, like me, are trying to be free. Then why not I teach them a lesson?" He then dressed himself in the best suit, hung his own worn-out and tattered garments on the same chair, and silently passed through the window to the piazza, and let himself down by one of the pillars, and started once more for the North.

Daylight came upon the fugitive before he had selected a hiding-place for the day, and he was walking at a rapid rate, in hopes of soon reaching some woodland or forest. The sun had just begun to show itself, when the fugitive was astounded at seeing behind him, in the distance, two men upon horseback. Taking a road to the right, the slave saw before him a farmhouse, and so near was he to it that he observed two men in front of it looking at him. It was too late to turn back. The kidnappers were behind him--strange men before him. Those in the rear he knew to be enemies, while he had no idea of what principles were the farmers. The latter also saw the white men coming, and called to the fugitive to come that way. The broad-brimmed hats that the farmers wore told the slave that they were Quakers.

Jerome had seen some of these people passing up and down the river, when employed on a steamer between Natchez and New Orleans, and had heard that they disliked slavery. He, therefore, hastened toward the drab-coated men, who, on his approach, opened the barn-door, and told him to "run in."

When Jerome entered the barn, the two farmers closed the door, remaining outside themselves, to confront the slave-catchers, who now came up and demanded admission, feeling that they had their prey secure.

"Thee can't enter my premises," said one of the Friends, in rather a musical voice.

The negro-catchers urged their claim to the slave, and intimated that, unless they were allowed to secure him, they would force their way in. By this time, several other Quakers had gathered around the barn-door. Unfortunately for the kidnappers, and most fortunately for the fugitive, the Friends had just been holding a quarterly meeting in the neighborhood, and a number of them had not yet returned to their homes.

After some talk, the men in drab promised to admit the hunters, provided they procured an officer and a search-warrant from a justice of the peace. One of the slave-catchers was left to see that the fugitive did not get away, while the others went in pursuit of an officer. In the mean time, the owner of the barn sent for a hammer and nails, and began nailing up the barn-door.

After an hour in search of the man of the law, they returned with an officer and a warrant. The Quaker demanded to see the paper, and, after looking at it for some time, called to his son to go into the house for his glasses. It was a long time before Aunt Ruth found the leather case, and when she did, the glasses wanted wiping before they could be used. After comfortably adjusting them on his nose, he read the warrant over leisurely.

"Come, Mr. Dugdale, we can't wait all day,'" said the officer.

"Well, will thee read it for me?" returned the Quaker.

The officer complied, and the man in drab said,--

"Yes, thee may go in, now. I am inclined to throw no obstacles in the way of the execution of the law of the land."

On approaching the door, the men found some forty or fifty nails in it, in the way of their progress.

"Lend me your hammer and a chisel, if you please, Mr. Dugdale," said the officer.

"Please read that paper over again, will thee?" asked the Quaker.

The officer once more read the warrant.

"I see nothing there which says I must furnish thee with tools to open my door. If thee wants a hammer, thee must go elsewhere for it; I tell thee plainly, thee can't have mine."

The implements for opening the door are at length obtained and after another half-hour, the slave-catchers are in the barn. Three hours is a long time for a slave to be in the hands of Quakers. The hay is turned over, and the barn is visited in every part; but still the runaway is not found. Uncle Joseph has a glow upon his countenance; Ephraim shakes his head knowingly; little Elijah is a perfect know-nothing, and, if you look toward the house, you will see Aunt Ruth's smiling face, ready to announce that breakfast is ready.

"The nigger is not in this barn," said the officer.

"I know he is not," quietly answered the Quaker.

"What were you nailing up your door for, then, as if you were afraid we would enter?" inquired one of the kidnappers.

"I can do what I please with my own door, can't I," said the Quaker.

The secret was out; the fugitive had gone in at the front door and out at the back; and the reading of the warrant, nailing up of the door, and other preliminaries of the Quaker, was to give the fugitive time and opportunity to escape.

It was now late in the morning, and the slave-catchers were a long way from home, and the horses were jaded by the rapid manner in which they had travelled. The Friends, in high glee, returned to the house for breakfast; the man of the law, after taking his fee, went home, and the kidnappers turned back, muttering, "Better luck next time."

CHAPTER XXI
SELF-SACRIFICE.

Now in her seventeenth year, Clotelle's personal appearance presented a great contrast to the time when she lived with old Mrs. Miller. Her tall and well-developed figure; her long, silky black hair, falling in curls down her swan-like neck; her bright, black eyes lighting up her olive-tinted face, and a set of teeth that a Tuscarora might envy, she was a picture of tropical-ripened beauty. At times, there was a heavenly smile upon her countenance, which would have warmed the heart of an anchorite. Such was the personal appearance of the girl who was now in prison by her own act to save the life of another. Would she be hanged in his stead, or would she receive a different kind of punishment? These questions Clotelle did not ask herself. Open, frank, free, and generous to a fault, she always thought of others, never of her own welfare.

The long stay of Clotelle caused some uneasiness to Miss Wilson; yet she dared not tell her father, for he had forbidden the slave-girl's going to the prison to see her lover. While the clock on the church near by was striking eleven, Georgiana called Sam, and sent him to the prison in search of Clotelle.

"The girl went away from here at eight o'clock," was the jailer's answer to the servant's inquiries.

The return of Sam without having found the girl saddened the heart of the young mistress. "Sure, then," said she, "the poor heart-broken thing has made way with herself."

Still, she waited till morning before breaking the news of Clotelle's absence to her father.

The jailer discovered, the next morning, to his utter astonishment, that his prisoner was white instead of black, and his first impression was that the change of complexion had taken place during the night, through fear of death. But this conjecture was soon dissipated; for the dark, glowing eyes, the sable curls upon the lofty brow, and the mild, sweet voice that answered his questions, informed him that the prisoner before him was another being.

On learning, in the morning, that Clotelle was in jail dressed in male attire, Miss Wilson immediately sent clothes to her to make a change in her attire. News of the heroic and daring act of the slave-girl spread through the city with electric speed.

"I will sell every nigger on the place," said the parson, at the break-fast-table,--"I will sell them all, and get a new lot, and whip them every day."

Poor Georgiana wept for the safety of Clotelle, while she felt glad that Jerome had escaped. In vain did they try to extort from the girl the whereabouts of the man whose escape she had effected. She was not aware that he had fled on a steamer, and when questioned, she replied,--

"I don't know; and if I did I would not tell you. I care not what you do with me, if Jerome but escapes."

The smile with which she uttered these words finely illustrated the poet's meaning, when he says,--

"A fearful gift upon thy heart is laid, Woman--the power to suffer and to love."

Her sweet simplicity seemed to dare them to lay their rough hands amid her trembling curls.

Three days did the heroic young woman remain in prison, to be gazed at by an unfeeling crowd, drawn there out of curiosity. The intelligence came to her at last that the court had decided to spare her life, on condition that she should be whipped, sold, and sent out of the State within twenty-four hours.

This order of the court she would have cared but little for, had she not been sincerely attached to her young mistress.

"Do try and sell her to some one who will use her well," said Georgiana to her father, as he was about taking his hat to leave the house.

"I shall not trouble myself to do any such thing," replied the hard-hearted parson. "I leave the finding of a master for her with the slave-dealer."

Bathed in tears, Miss. Wilson paced her room in the absence of her father. For many months Georgiana had been in a decline, and any little trouble would lay her on a sick bed for days. She was, therefore, poorly able to bear the loss of this companion, whom she so dearly loved.

Mr. Wilson had informed his daughter that Clotelle was to be flogged; and when Felice came in and informed her mistress that the poor girl had just received fifty lashes on her bare person, the young lady fainted and fell on the floor. The servants placed their mistress on the sofa, and went in pursuit of their master. Little did the preacher think, on returning to his daughter, that he should soon be bereft of her; yet such was to be his lot. A blood-vessel had been ruptured, and the three physicians who were called in told the father that he must prepare to lose his child. That moral courage and calmness, which was her great characteristic, did not forsake Georgiana in her hour of death. She had ever been kind to the slaves under her charge, and they loved and respected her. At her request, the servants were all brought into her room, and took a last farewell of their mistress. Seldom, if ever, was there witnessed a more touching scene than this. There lay the young woman, pale and feeble, with death stamped upon her countenance, surrounded by the sons and daughters of Africa, some of whom had been separated from every earthly tie, and the most of whose persons had been torn and gashed by the negro-whip. Some were upon their knees at the bedside, others standing around, and all weeping.

Death is a leveler; and neither age, sex, wealth, nor condition, can avert when he is permitted to strike. The most beautiful flowers must soon fade and droop and die. So, also, with man; his days are as uncertain as the passing breeze. This hour he glows in the blush of health and vigor, but the next, he may be counted with the number no more known on earth. Oh, what a silence pervaded the house when this young flower was gone! In the midst of the buoyancy of youth, this cherished one had drooped and died. Deep were the sounds of grief and mourning heard in that stately dwelling when the stricken friends, whose office it had been to nurse and soothe the weary sufferer, beheld her pale and motionless in the sleep of death.

Who can imagine the feeling with which poor Clotelle received the intelligence of her kind friend's death? The deep gashes of the cruel whip had prostrated the lovely form of the quadroon, and she lay upon her bed of straw in the dark cell. The speculator had bought her, but had postponed her removal till she should recover. Her benefactress was dead, and--

"Hope withering fled, and mercy sighed farewell."

"Is Jerome safe?" she would ask herself continually. If her lover could have but known of the sufferings of that sweet flower,--that polyanthus over which he had so often been in his dreams,--he would then have learned that she was worthy of his love.

It was more than a fortnight before the slave-trader could take his prize to more comfortable quarters. Like Alcibiades, who defaced the images of the gods and expected to be pardoned on the ground of eccentricity, so men who abuse God's image hope to escape the vengeance of his wrath under the plea that the law sanctions their atrocious deeds.

CHAPTER XXII
LOVE AT FIRST SIGHT AND WHAT FOLLOWED.

It was a beautiful Sunday in September, with a cloudless sky, and the rays of the sun parching the already thirsty earth, that Clotelle stood at an upper window in Slater's slave-pen in New Orleans, gasping for a breath of fresh air. The bells of thirty churches were calling the people to the different places of worship. Crowds were seen wending their way to the houses of God; one followed by a negro boy carrying his master's Bible; another followed by her maid-servant holding the mistress' fan; a third supporting an umbrella over his master's head to shield him from the burning sun. Baptists immersed, Presbyterians sprinkled, Methodists shouted, and Episcopalians read their prayers, while ministers of the various sects preached that Christ died for all. The chiming of the bells seemed to mock the sighs and deep groans of the forty human beings then incarcerated in the slave-pen. These imprisoned children of God were many of them Methodists, some Baptists, and others claiming to believe in the faith of the Presbyterians and Episcopalians.

Oh, with what anxiety did these creatures await the close of that Sabbath, and the dawn of another day, that should deliver them from those dismal and close cells. Slowly the day passed away, and once more the evening breeze found its way through the barred windows of the prison that contained these injured sons and daughters of America. The clock on the calaboose had just struck nine on Monday morning, when hundreds of persons were seen threading the gates and doors of the negro-pen. It was the same gang that had the day previous been stepping to the tune and keeping time with the musical church bells. Their Bibles were not with them, their prayer-books were left at home, and even their long and solemn faces had been laid aside for the week. They had come to the man-market to make their purchases. Methodists were in search of their brethren. Baptists were looking for those that had been immersed, while Presbyterians were willing to buy fellow Christians, whether sprinkled or not. The crowd was soon gazing at and feasting their eyes upon the lovely features of Clotelle.

"She is handsomer," muttered one to himself, "than the lady that sat in the pew next to me yesterday."

"I would that my daughter was half so pretty," thinks a second.

Groups are seen talking in every part of the vast building, and the topic on 'Change, is the "beautiful quadroon." By and by, a tall young man with a foreign face, the curling mustache protruding from under a finely-chiseled nose, and having the air of a gentleman, passes by. His dark hazel eye is fastened on the maid, and he stops for a moment; the stranger walks away, but soon returns--he looks, he sees the young woman wipe away the silent tear that steals down her alabaster cheek; he feels ashamed that he should gaze so unmanly on the blushing face of the woman. As he turns upon his heel he takes out his white hankerchief and wipes his eyes. It may be that he has lost a sister, a mother, or some dear one to whom he was betrothed. Again he comes, and the quadroon hides her face. She has heard that foreigners make bad masters, and she shuns his piercing gaze. Again he goes away and then returns. He takes a last look and then walks hurriedly off.

The day wears away, but long before the time of closing the sale the tall young man once more enters the slave-pen. He looks in every direction for the beautiful slave, but she is not there--she has been sold! He goes to the trader and inquires, but he is too late, and he therefore returns to his hotel.

Having entered a military school in Paris when quite young, and soon after been sent with the French army to India, Antoine Devenant had never dabbled in matters of love. He viewed all women from the same stand-point--respected them for their virtues, and often spoke of the goodness of heart of the sex, but never dreamed of taking to himself a wife. The unequalled beauty of Clotelle had dazzled his eyes, and every look that she gave was a dagger that went to his heart. He felt a shortness of breath, his heart palpitated, his head grew dizzy, and his limbs trembled; but he knew not its cause. This was the first stage of "love at first sight."

He who bows to the shrine of beauty when beckoned by this mysterious agent seldom regrets it. Devenant reproached himself for not having made inquiries concerning the girl before he left the market in the morning. His stay in the city was to be short, and the yellow fever was raging, which caused him to feel like making a still earlier departure. The disease appeared in a form unusually severe and repulsive. It seized its victims from amongst the most healthy of the citizens. The disorder began in the brain by oppressive pain accompanied or followed by fever. Fiery veins streaked the eye, the face was inflamed and dyed of a dark dull red color; the ears from time to time rang painfully. Now mucous secretions surcharged the tongue and took away the power of speech; now the sick one spoke, but in speaking had foresight of death. When the violence of the disease approached the heart, the gums were blackened. The sleep broken, troubled by convulsions, or by frightful visions, was worse than the waking hours; and when the reason sank under a delirium which had its seat in the brain, repose utterly forsook the patient's couch. The progress of the fever within was marked by yellowish spots, which spread over the surface of the body. If then, a happy crisis came not, all hope was gone. Soon the breath infected the air with a fetid odor, the lips were glazed, despair painted itself in the eyes, and sobs, with long intervals of silence, formed the only language. From each side of the mouth, spread foam tinged with black and burnt blood. Blue streaks mingled with the yellow all over the frame. All remedies were useless. This was the yellow fever. The disorder spread alarm and confusion throughout the city.

On an average more than four hundred died daily. In the midst of disorder and confusion, death heaped victims on victims. Friend followed friend in quick succession. The sick were avoided from the fear of contagion, and for the same reason the dead were left unburied. Nearly two thousand dead bodies lay uncovered in the burial-ground, with only here and there a little lime thrown over them, to prevent the air becoming infected. The negro, whose home is in a hot climate, was not proof against the disease. Many plantations had to suspend their work for want of slaves to take the places of those who had been taken off by the fever.

CHAPTER XXIII
MEETING OF THE COUSINS.

The clock in the hall had scarcely finished striking three when Mr. Taylor entered his own dwelling, a fine residence in Camp Street, New Orleans, followed by the slave-girl whom he had just purchased at the negro-pen. Clotelle looked around wildly as she passed through the hall into the presence of her new mistress. Mrs. Taylor was much pleased with her servant's appearance, and congratulated her husband on his judicious choice.

"But," said Mrs. Taylor, after Clotelle had gone into the kitchen, "how much she looks like Miss Jane Morton."

"Indeed," replied the husband, "I thought, the moment I saw her that she looked like the Mortons."

"I am sure I never saw two faces more alike in my life, than that girl's and Jane Morton's," continued Mrs. Taylor.

Dr. Morton, the purchaser of Maron, the youngest daughter of Agnes, and sister to Isabella, had resided in Camp Street, near the Taylors, for more than eight years, and the families were on very intimate terms, and visited each other frequently. Every one spoke of Clotelle's close resemblance to the Mortons, and especially to the eldest daughter. Indeed, two sisters could hardly have been more alike. The large, dark eyes, black, silk-like hair, tall, graceful figure, and mould of the face, were the same.

The morning following Clotelle's arrival in her new home, Mrs. Taylor was conversing in a low tone with her husband, and both with their eyes following Clotelle as she passed through the room.

"She is far above the station of a slave," remarked the lady. "I saw her, last night, when removing some books, open one and stand over it a moment as if she was reading; and she is as white as I am. I almost sorry you bought her."

At this juncture the front door-bell rang, and Clotelle hurried through the room to answer it.

"Miss Morton," said the servant as she returned to the mistress' room.

"Ask her to walk in," responded the mistress.

"Now, my dear," said Mrs. Taylor to her husband, "just look and see if you do not notice a marked resemblance between the countenances of Jane and Clotelle."

Miss Morton entered the room just as Mrs. Taylor ceased speaking.

"Have you heard that the Jamisons are down with the fever?" inquired the young lady, after asking about the health of the Taylors.

"No, I had not; I was in hopes it would not get into our street;" replied Mrs. Taylor.

All this while Mr. and Mrs. Taylor were keenly scrutinizing their visitor and Clotelle and even the two young women seemed to be conscious that they were in some way the objects of more than usual attention.

Miss Morton had scarcely departed before Mrs. Taylor began questioning Clotelle concerning her early childhood, and became more than ever satisfied that the slave-girl was in some way connected with the Mortons.

Every hour brought fresh news of the ravages of the fever, and the Taylors commenced preparing to leave town. As Mr. Taylor could not go at once, it was determined that his wife should leave without him, accompanied by her new maid servant. Just as Mrs. Taylor and Clotelle were stepping into the carriage, they were informed that Dr. Morton was down with the epidemic.

It was a beautiful day, with a fine breeze for the time of year, that Mrs. Taylor and her servant found themselves in the cabin of the splendid new steamer "Walk-in-the-Water," bound from New Orleans to Mobile. Every berth in the boat wad occupied by persons fleeing from the fearful contagion that was carrying off its hundreds daily.

Late in the day, as Clotelle was standing at one of the windows of the ladies' saloon, she was astonished to see near her, and with eyes fixed intently upon her, the tall young stranger whom she had observed in the slave-market a few days before. She turned hastily away, but the heated cabin and the want of fresh air soon drove her again to the window. The young gentleman again appeared, and coming to the end of the saloon, spoke to the slave-girl in broken English. This confirmed her in her previous opinion that he was a foreigner, and she rejoiced that she had not fallen into his hands.

"I want to talk with you," said the stranger.

"What do you want with me?" she inquired.

"I am your friend," he answered. "I saw you in the slave-market last week, and regretted that I did not speak to you then. I returned in the evening, but you was gone."

Clotelle looked indignantly at the stranger, and was about leaving the window again when the quivering of his lips and the trembling of his voice struck her attention and caused her to remain.

"I intended to buy you and make you free and happy, but I was too late," continued he.

"Why do you wish to make me free?" inquired the girl.

"Because I once had an only and lovely sister, who died three years ago in France, and you are so much like her that had I not known of her death I should certainly have taken you for her."

"However much I may resemble your sister, you are aware that I am not she; why, then, take so much interest in one whom you have never seen before and may never see again?"

"The love," said he, "which I had for my sister is transferred to you."

Clotelle had all along suspected that the man was a knave, and this profession of love at once confirmed her in that belief. She therefore immediately turned away and left him.

Hours elapsed. Twilight was just "letting down her curtain and pinning it with a star," as the slave-girl seated herself on a sofa by the window, and began meditating upon her eventful history, meanwhile watching the white waves as they seemed to sport with each other in the wake of the noble vessel, with the rising moon reflecting its silver rays upon the splendid scene, when the foreigner once more appeared near the window. Although agitated for fear her mistress would see her talking to a stranger, and be angry, Clotelle still thought she saw something in the countenance of the young man that told her he was sincere, and she did not wish to hurt his feelings.

"Why persist in your wish to talk with me?" she said, as he again advanced and spoke to her.

"I wish to purchase you and make you happy," returned he.

"But I am not for sale now," she replied. "My present mistress will not sell me, and if you wished to do so ever so much you could not."

"Then," said he, "if I cannot buy you, when the steamer reaches Mobile, fly with me, and you shall be free."

"I cannot do it," said Clotelle; and she was just leaving the stranger when he took from his pocket a piece of paper and thrust it into her hand.

After returning to her room, she unfolded the paper, and found, to her utter astonishment that it contained a one hundred dollar note on the Bank of the United States. The first impulse of the girl was to return the paper and its contents immediately to the giver, but examining the paper more closely, she saw in faint pencil-marks, "Remember this is from one who loves you." Another thought was to give it to her mistress, and she returned to the saloon for that purpose; but on finding Mrs. Taylor engaged in conversation with some ladies, she did not deem it proper to interrupt her.

Again, therefore, Clotelle seated herself by the window, and again the stranger presented himself. She immediately took the paper from her pocket, and handed it to him; but he declined taking it, saying,--

"No, keep it; it may be of some service to you when I am far away."

"Would that I could understand you," said the slave.

"Believe that I am sincere, and then you will understand me," returned the young man. "Would you rather be a slave than be free?" inquired he, with tears that glistened in the rays of the moon.

"No," said she, "I want my freedom, but I must live a virtuous life."

"Then, if you would be free and happy, go with me. We shall be in Mobile in two hours, and when the passengers are going on shore, you take my arm. Have your face covered with a veil, and you will not be observed. We will take passage immediately for France; you can pass as my sister, and I pledge you my honor that I will marry you as soon as we arrive in France."

This solemn promise, coupled with what had previously been said, gave Clotelle confidence in the man, and she instantly determined to go with him. "But then," thought she, "what if I should be detected? I would be forever ruined, for I would be sold, and in all probability have to end my days on a cotton, rice, or sugar plantation." However, the thought of freedom in the future outweighed this danger, and her resolve was taken.

Dressing herself in some of her best clothes, and placing her veiled bonnet where she could get it without the knowledge of her mistress, Clotelle awaited with a heart filled with the deepest emotions and anxiety the moment when she was to take a step which seemed so rash, and which would either make or ruin her forever.

The ships which leave Mobile for Europe lie about thirty miles down the bay, and passengers are taken down from the city in small vessels. The "Walk-in-the-Water" had just made her lines fast, and the passengers were hurrying on shore, when a tall gentleman with a lady at his side descended the stage-plank, and stepped on the wharf. This was Antoine Devenant and Clotelle.

CHAPTER XXIV
THE LAW AND ITS VICTIM.

The death of Dr. Morton, on the third day of his illness, came like a shock upon his wife and daughters. The corpse had scarcely been committed to its mother earth before new and unforeseen difficulties appeared to them. By the laws of the Slave States, the children follow the condition of their mother. If the mother is free, the children are free; if a slave, the children are slaves. Being unacquainted with the Southern code, and no one presuming that Marion had any negro blood in her veins, Dr. Morton had not given the subject a single thought. The woman whom he loved and regarded as his wife was, after all, nothing more than a slave by the laws of the State. What would have been his feelings had he known that at his death his wife and children would be considered as his property? Yet such was the case. Like most men of means at that time, Dr. Morton was deeply engaged in speculation, and though generally considered wealthy, was very much involved in his business affairs.

After the disease with which Dr. Morton had so suddenly died had to some extent subsided, Mr. James Morton, a brother of the deceased, went to New Orleans to settle up the estate. On his arrival there, he was pleased with and felt proud of his nieces, and invited them to return with him to Vermont, little dreaming that his brother had married a slave, and that his widow and daughters would be claimed as such. The girls themselves had never heard that their mother had been a slave, and therefore knew nothing of the danger hanging over their heads.

An inventory of the property of the deceased was made out by Mr. Morton, and placed in the hands of the creditors. These preliminaries being arranged, the ladies, with their relative, concluded to leave the city and reside for a few days on the banks of Lake Ponchartrain, where they could enjoy a fresh air that the city did not afford. As they were about taking the cars, however, an officer arrested the whole party--the ladies as slaves, and the gentleman upon the charge of attempting to conceal the property of his deceased brother. Mr. Morton was overwhelmed with horror at the idea of his nieces being claimed as slaves, and asked for time, that he might save them from such a fate. He even offered to mortgage his little farm in Vermont for the amount which young slave-women of their ages would fetch. But the creditors pleaded that they were an "extra article," and would sell for more than common slaves, and must therefore be sold at auction.

The uncle was therefore compelled to give them up to the officers of the law, and they were separated from him. Jane, the oldest of the girls, as we have before mentioned, was very handsome, bearing a close resemblance to her cousin Clotelle. Alreka, though not as handsome as her sister, was nevertheless a beautiful girl, and both had all the accomplishments that wealth and station could procure.

Though only in her fifteenth year, Alreka had become strongly attached to Volney Lapie, a young Frenchman, a student in her father's office. This attachment was reciprocated, although the poverty of the young man and the extreme youth of the girl had caused their feelings to be kept from the young lady's parents.

The day of sale came, and Mr. Morton attended, with the hope that either the magnanimity of the creditors or his own little farm in Vermont might save his nieces from the fate that awaited them. His hope, however, was in vain. The feelings of all present seemed to be lost in the general wish to become the possessor of the young ladies, who stood trembling, blushing, and weeping as the numerous throng gazed at them, or as the intended purchaser examined the graceful proportions of their fair and beautiful frames. Neither the presence of the uncle nor young Lapie could at all lessen the gross language of the officers, or stay the rude hands of those who wished to examine the property thus offered for sale. After a fierce contest between the bidders, the girls were sold, one for two thousand three hundred, and the other for two thousand three hundred and fifty dollars. Had these girls been bought for servants only, they would in all probability have brought not more than nine hundred or a thousand dollars each. Here were two beautiful young girls, accustomed to the fondest indulgence, surrounded by all the refinements of life, and with the timidity and gentleness which such a life would naturally produce, bartered away like cattle in the markets of Smithfield or New York.

The mother, who was also to have been sold, happily followed her husband to the grave, and was spared the pangs of a broken heart.

The purchaser of the young ladies left the market in triumph, and the uncle, with a heavy heart, started for his New England home, with no earthly prospect of ever beholding his nieces again.

The seizure of the young ladies as slaves was the result of the administrator's having found among Dr. Morton's papers the bill-of-sale of Marion which he had taken when he purchased her. He had doubtless intended to liberate her when he married her, but had neglected from time to time to have the proper papers made out. Sad was the result of this negligence.

CHAPTER XXV
THE FLIGHT.

On once gaining the wharf, Devenant and Clotelle found no difficulty in securing an immediate passage to France. The fine packet-ship Utica lay down the bay, and only awaited the return of the lighter that night to complete her cargo and list of passengers, ere she departed. The young Frenchman therefore took his prize on board, and started for the ship.

Daylight was just making its appearance the next morning when the Utica weighed anchor and turned her prow toward the sea. In the course of three hours, the vessel, with outspread sails, was rapidly flying from land. Everything appeared to be auspicious. The skies were beautifully clear, and the sea calm, with a sun that dazzled the whole scene. But clouds soon began to chase each other through the heavens and the sea became rough. It was then that Clotelle felt that there was hope of escaping. She had hitherto kept in the cabin, but now she expressed a wish to come on deck. The hanging clouds were narrowing the horizon to a span, and gloomily mingling with the rising surges. The old and grave-looking seamen shook their weather-wise heads as if foretelling a storm.

As Clotelle came on deck, she strained her eyes in vain to catch a farewell view of her native land. With a smile on her countenance, but with her eyes filled with tears, she said,--

"Farewell, farewell to the land of my birth, and welcome, welcome, ye dark blue waves. I care not where I go, so it is

'Where a tyrant never trod,   Where a slave was never known,   But where nature worships God,   If in the wilderness alone.'"

Devenant stood by her side, seeming proud of his future wife, with his face in a glow at his success, while over his noble brow clustering locks of glossy black hair were hanging in careless ringlets. His finely-cut, classic features wore the aspect of one possessed with a large and noble heart.

Once more the beautiful Clotelle whispered in the ear of her lover,--

"Away, away, o'er land and sea,   America is now no home for me."

The winds increased with nightfall, and impenetrable gloom surrounded the ship. The prospect was too uncheering, even to persons in love. The attention which Devenant paid to Clotelle, although she had been registered on the ship's passenger list as his sister, caused more than one to look upon his as an agreeable travelling companion. His tall, slender figure and fine countenance bespoke for him at first sight one's confidence. That he was sincerely and deeply enamored of Clotelle all could see.

The weather became still more squally. The wind rushed through the white, foaming waves, and the ship groaned with its own wild and ungovernable labors, while nothing could be seen but the wild waste of waters. The scene was indeed one of fearful sublimity.

Day came and went without any abatement of the storm. Despair was now on every countenance. Occasionally a vivid flash of lightning would break forth and illuminate the black and boiling surges that surrounded the vessel, which was now scudding before the blast under bare poles.

After five days of most intensely stormy weather, the sea settled down into a dead calm, and the passengers flocked on deck. During the last three days of the storm, Clotelle had been so unwell as to be unable to raise her head. Her pale face and quivering lips and languid appearance made her look as if every pulsation had ceased. Her magnificent large and soft eyes, fringed with lashes as dark as night, gave her an angelic appearance. The unreserved attention of Devenant, even when sea-sick himself, did much to increase the little love that the at first distrustful girl had placed in him. The heart must always have some object on which to centre its affections, and Clotelle having lost all hope of ever again seeing Jerome, it was but natural that she should now transfer her love to one who was so greatly befriending her. At first she respected Devenant for the love he manifested for her, and for his apparent willingness to make any sacrifice for her welfare. True, this was an adventure upon which she had risked her all, and should her heart be foiled in this search for hidden treasures, her affections would be shipwrecked forever. She felt under great obligations to the man who had thus effected her escape, and that noble act alone would entitle him to her love.

Each day became more pleasant as the noble ship sped onward amid the rippled spray. The whistling of the breeze through the rigging was music to the ear, and brought gladness to the heart of every one on board. At last, the long suspense was broken by the appearance of land, at which all hearts leaped for joy. It was a beautiful morning in October. The sun had just risen, and sky and earth were still bathed in his soft, rosy glow, when the Utica hauled into the dock at Bordeaux. The splendid streets, beautiful bridges, glittering equipages, and smiling countenances of the people, gave everything a happy appearance, after a voyage of twenty-nine days on the deep, deep sea.

After getting their baggage cleared from the custom-house and going to a hotel, Devenant made immediate arrangements for the marriage. Clotelle, on arriving at the church where the ceremony was to take place, was completely overwhelmed at the spectacle. She had never beheld a scene so gorgeous as this. The magnificent dresses of the priests and choristers, the deep and solemn voices, the elevated crucifix, the burning tapers, the splendidly decorated altar, the sweet-smelling incense, made the occasion truly an imposing one. At the conclusion of the ceremony, the loud and solemn peals of the organ's swelling anthem were lost to all in the contemplation of the interesting scene.

The happy couple set out at once for Dunkirk, the residence of the bridegroom's parents. But their stay there was short, for they had scarcely commenced visiting the numerous friends of the husband ere orders came for him to proceed to India to join that portion of the French army then stationed there.

In due course of time they left for India, passing through Paris and Lyons, taking ship at Marseilles. In the metropolis of France, they spent a week, where the husband took delight in introducing his wife to his brother officers in the French army, and where the newly-married couple were introduced to Louis Phillippe, then King of France. In all of these positions, Clotelle sustained herself in a most ladylike manner.

At Lyons, they visited the vast factories and other public works, and all was pleasure with them. The voyage from Marseilles to Calcutta was very pleasant, as the weather was exceedingly fine. On arriving in India, Captain Devenant and lady were received with honors--the former for his heroic bravery in more than one battle, and the latter for her fascinating beauty and pleasing manners, and the fact that she was connected with one who was a general favorite with all who had his acquaintance. This was indeed a great change for Clotelle. Six months had not elapsed since her exposure in the slave-market of New Orleans. This life is a stage, and we are indeed all actors.

CHAPTER XXVI
THE HERO OF A NIGHT.

Mounted on a fast horse, with the Quaker's son for a guide, Jerome pressed forward while Uncle Joseph was detaining the slave-catchers at the barn-door, through which the fugitive had just escaped. When out of present danger, fearing that suspicion might be aroused if he continued on the road in open day, Jerome buried himself in a thick, dark forest until nightfall. With a yearning heart, he saw the splendor of the setting sun lingering on the hills, as if loath to fade away and be lost in the more sombre hues of twilight, which, rising from the east, was slowly stealing over the expanse of heaven, bearing silence and repose, which should cover his flight from a neighborhood to him so full of dangers.

Wearily and alone, with nothing but the hope of safety before him to cheer him on his way, the poor fugitive urged his tired and trembling limbs forward for several nights. The new suit of clothes with which he had provided himself when he made his escape from his captors, and the twenty dollars which the young Quaker had slipped into his hand, when bidding him "Fare thee well," would enable him to appear genteelly as soon as he dared to travel by daylight, and would thus facilitate his progress toward freedom.

It was late in the evening when the fugitive slave arrived at a small town on the banks of Lake Erie, where he was to remain over night. How strange were his feelings! While his heart throbbed for that freedom and safety which Canada alone could furnish to the whip-scarred slave, on the American continent, his thoughts were with Clotelle. Was she still in prison, and if so, what would be her punishment for aiding him to escape from prison? Would he ever behold her again? These were the thoughts that followed him to his pillow, haunted him in is dreams, and awakened him from his slumbers.

The alarm of fire aroused the inmates of the hotel in which Jerome had sought shelter for the night from the deep sleep into which they had fallen. The whole village was buried in slumber, and the building was half consumed before the frightened inhabitants had reached the scene of the conflagration. The wind was high, and the burning embers were wafted like so many rockets through the sky. The whole town was lighted up, and the cries of women and children in the streets made the scene a terrific one. Jerome heard the alarm, and hastily dressing himself, he went forth and hastened toward the burning building.

"There,--there in that room in the second story, is my child!" exclaimed a woman, wringing her hands, and imploring some one to go to the rescue of her little one.

The broad sheets of fire were flying in the direction of the chamber in which the child was sleeping, and all hope of its being saved seemed gone. Occasionally the wind would lift the pall of smoke, and show that the work of destruction was not yet complete. At last a long ladder was brought, and one end placed under the window of the room. A moment more and a bystander mounted the ladder and ascended in haste to the window. The smoke met him as he raised the sash, and he cried out, "All is lost!" and returned to the ground without entering the room.

Another sweep of the wind showed that the destroying element had not yet made its final visit to that part of the doomed building. The mother, seeing that all hope of again meeting her child in this world was gone, wrung her hands and seemed inconsolable with grief.

At this juncture, a man was seen to mount the ladder, and ascend with great rapidity. All eyes were instantly turned to the figure of this unknown individual as it disappeared in the cloud of smoke escaping from the window. Those who a moment before had been removing furniture, as well as the idlers who had congregated at the ringing of the bells, assembled at the foot of the ladder, and awaited with breathless silence the reappearance of the stranger, who, regardless of his own safety, had thus risked his life to save another's. Three cheers broke the stillness that had fallen on the company, as the brave man was seen coming through the window and slowly descending to the ground, holding under one arm the inanimate form of the child. Another cheer, and then another, made the welkin ring, as the stranger, with hair burned and eyebrows closely singed, fainted at the foot of the ladder. But the child was saved.

The stranger was Jerome. As soon as he revived, he shrunk from every eye, as if he feared they would take from him the freedom which he had gone through so much to obtain.

The next day, the fugitive took a vessel, and the following morning found himself standing on the free soil of Canada. As his foot pressed the shore, he threw himself upon his face, kissed the earth, and exclaimed, "O God! I thank thee that I am a free man."

CHAPTER XXVII
TRUE FREEDOM.

The history of the African race is God's illuminated clock, set in the dark steeple of time. The negro has been made the hewer of wood and the drawer of water for nearly all other nations. The people of the United States, however, will have an account to settle with God, owing to their treatment of the negro, which will far surpass the rest of mankind.

Jerome, on reaching Canada, felt for the first time that personal freedom which God intended that all who bore his image should enjoy. That same forgetfulness of self which had always characterized him now caused him to think of others. The thoughts of dear ones in slavery were continually in his mind, and above all others, Clotelle occupied his thoughts. Now that he was free, he could better appreciate her condition as a slave. Although Jerome met, on his arrival in Canada, numbers who had escaped from the Southern States, he nevertheless shrank from all society, particularly that of females. The soft, silver-gray tints on the leaves of the trees, with their snow-spotted trunks, and a biting air, warned the new-born freeman that he was in another climate. Jerome sought work, and soon found it; and arranged with his employer that the latter should go to Natchez in search of Clotelle. The good Scotchman, for whom the fugitive was laboring, freely offered to go down and purchase the girl, if she could be bought, and let Jerome pay him in work. With such a prospect of future happiness in view, this injured descendant of outraged and bleeding Africa went daily to his toil with an energy hitherto unknown to him. But oh, how vain are the hopes of man!

CHAPTER XXVIII
FAREWELL TO AMERICA.

Three months had elapsed, from the time the fugitive commenced work for

Mr. Streeter, when that gentleman returned from his Southern research, and informed Jerome that Parson Wilson had sold Clotelle, and that she had been sent to the New Orleans slave-market.

This intelligence fell with crushing weight upon the heart of Jerome, and he now felt that the last chain which bound him to his native land was severed. He therefore determined to leave America forever. His nearest and dearest friends had often been flogged in his very presence, and he had seen his mother sold to the negro-trader. An only sister had been torn from him by the soul-driver; he had himself been sold and resold, and been compelled to submit to the most degrading and humiliating insults; and now that the woman upon whom his heart doted, and without whom life was a burden, had been taken away forever, he felt it a duty to hate all mankind.

If there is one thing more than another calculated to make one hate and detest American slavery, it is to witness the meetings between fugitives and their friends in Canada. Jerome had beheld some of these scenes. The wife who, after years of separation, had escaped from her prison-house and followed her husband had told her story to him. He had seen the newly-arrived wife rush into the arms of the husband, whose dark face she had not looked upon for long, weary years. Some told of how a sister had been ill-used by the overseer; others of a husband's being whipped to death for having attempted to protect his wife. He had sat in the little log-hut, by the fireside, and heard tales that caused his heart to bleed; and his bosom swelled with just indignation when he thought that there was no remedy for such atrocious acts. It was with such feelings that he informed his employer that he should leave him at the expiration of a month.

In vain did Mr. Streeter try to persuade Jerome to remain with him; and late, in the month of February, the latter found himself on board a small vessel loaded with pine-lumber, descending the St. Lawrence, bound for Liverpool. The bark, though an old one, was, nevertheless, considered seaworthy, and the fugitive was working his way out. As the vessel left the river and gained the open sea, the black man appeared to rejoice at the prospect of leaving a country in which his right to manhood had been denied him, and his happiness destroyed.

The wind was proudly swelling the white sails, and the little craft plunging into the foaming waves, with the land fast receding in the distance, when Jerome mounted a pile of lumber to take a last farewell of his native land. With tears glistening in his eyes, and with quivering lips, he turned his gaze toward the shores that were fast fading in the dim distance, and said,--

"Though forced from my native land by the tyrants of the South, I hope I shall some day be able to return. With all her faults, I love my country still."

CHAPTER XXIX
A STRANGER IN A STRANGE LAND.

The rain was falling on the dirty pavements of Liverpool as Jerome left the vessel after her arrival. Passing the custom-house, he took a cab, and proceeded to Brown's Hotel, Clayton Square.

Finding no employment in Liverpool, Jerome determined to go into the interior and seek for work. He, therefore, called for his bill, and made ready for his departure. Although but four days at the Albion, he found the hotel charges larger than he expected; but a stranger generally counts on being "fleeced" in travelling through the Old World, and especially in Great Britain. After paying his bill, he was about leaving the room, when one of the servants presented himself with a low bow, and said,--

"Something for the waiter, sir?"

"I thought I had paid my bill," replied the man, somewhat surprised at this polite dun.

"I am the waiter, sir, and gets only what strangers see fit to give me."

Taking from his pocket his nearly empty purse, Jerome handed the man a half-crown; but he had hardly restored it to his pocket, before his eye fell on another man in the waiting costume.

"What do you want?" he asked.

"Whatever your honor sees fit to give me, sir. I am the tother waiter."

The purse was again taken from the pocket, and another half-crown handed out. Stepping out into the hall, he saw standing there a good-looking woman, in a white apron, who made a very pretty courtesy.

"What's your business?" he inquired.

"I am the chambermaid, sir, and looks after the gentlemen's beds."

Out came the purse again, and was relieved of another half-crown; whereupon another girl, with a fascinating smile, took the place of the one who had just received her fee.

"What do you want?" demanded the now half-angry Jerome.

"Please, sir, I am the tother chambermaid."

Finding it easier to give shillings than half-crowns, Jerome handed the woman a shilling, and again restored his purse to his pocket, glad that another woman was not to be seen.

Scarcely had he commenced congratulating himself, however, before three men made their appearance, one after another.

"What have you done for me?" he asked of the first.

"I am the boots, sir."

The purse came out once more, and a shilling was deposited in the servant's hand.

"What do I owe you?" he inquired of the second.

"I took your honor's letter to the post, yesterday, sir."

Another shilling left the purse.

"In the name of the Lord, what am I indebted to you for?" demanded Jerome, now entirely out of patience, turning to the last of the trio.

"I told yer vership vot time it vas, this morning."

"Well!" exclaimed the indignant man, "ask here what o'clock it is, and you have got to pay for it."

He paid this last demand with a sixpence, regretting that he had not commenced with sixpences instead of half-crowns.

Having cleared off all demands in the house, he started for the railway station; but had scarcely reached the street, before he was accosted by an old man with a broom in his hand, who, with an exceedingly low bow, said,--

"I is here, yer lordship."

"I did not send for you; what is your business?" demanded Jerome.

"I is the man what opened your lordship's cab-door, when your lordship came to the house on Monday last, and I know your honor won't allow a poor man to starve."

Putting a sixpence in the old man's hand, Jerome once more started for the depot. Having obtained letters of introduction to persons in Manchester, he found no difficulty in getting a situation in a large manufacturing house there. Although the salary was small, yet the situation was a much better one than he had hoped to obtain. His compensation as out-door clerk enabled him to employ a man to teach him at night, and, by continued study and attention to business, he was soon promoted.

After three years in his new home, Jerome was placed in a still higher position, where his salary amounted to fifteen hundred dollars a year. The drinking, smoking, and other expensive habits, which the clerks usually indulged in, he carefully avoided.

Being fond of poetry, he turned his attention to literature. Johnson's "Lives of the Poets," the writings of Dryden, Addison, Pope, Clarendon, and other authors of celebrity, he read with attention. The knowledge which he thus picked up during his leisure hours gave him a great advantage over the other clerks, and caused his employers to respect him far more than any other in their establishment. So eager was he to improve the time that he determined to see how much he could read during the unemployed time of night and morning, and his success was beyond his expectations.

CHAPTER XXX
NEW FRIENDS.

Broken down in health, after ten years of close confinement in his situation, Jerome resolved to give it up, and thereby release himself from an employment which seemed calculated to send him to a premature grave.

It was on a beautiful morning in summer that he started for Scotland, having made up his mind to travel for his health. After visiting Edinburgh and Glasgow, he concluded to spend a few days in the old town of Perth, with a friend whose acquaintance he had made in Manchester. During the second day of his stay in Perth, while crossing the main street, Jerome saw a pony-chaise coming toward him with great speed. A lady, who appeared to be the only occupant of the vehicle, was using her utmost strength to stop the frightened horses. The footman, in his fright, had leaped from behind the carriage, and was following with the crowd. With that self-forgetfulness which was one of his chief characteristics, Jerome threw himself before the horses to stop them; and, seizing the high-spirited animals by the bit, as they dashed by him, he was dragged several rods before their speed was checked, which was not accomplished until one of the horses had fallen to the ground, with the heroic man struggling beneath him.

All present were satisfied that this daring act alone had saved the lady's life, for the chaise must inevitably have been dashed in pieces, had the horses not been thus suddenly checked in their mad career.

On the morning following this perilous adventure, Col. G----called at Jerome's temporary residence, and, after expressing his admiration for his noble daring, and thanking him for having saved his daughter's life, invited him to visit him at his country residence. This invitation was promptly accepted in the spirit in which it was given; and three days after, Jerome found himself at the princely residence of the father of the lady for whose safety he had risked his own life. The house was surrounded by fine trees, and a sweet little stream ran murmuring at the foot, while beds of flowers on every hand shed their odors on the summer air. It was, indeed, a pleasant place to spend the warm weather, and the colonel and his family gave Jerome a most cordial welcome. Miss G. showed especial attention to the stranger. He had not intended remaining longer than the following day: but the family insisted on his taking part in a fox-hunt that was to come off on the morning of the third day. Wishing to witness a scene as interesting as the chase usually proves to be, he decided to remain.

Fifteen persons, five of whom were ladies, were on the ground at the appointed hour. Miss G. was, of course, one of the party. In vain Jerome endeavored to excuse himself from joining in the chase. His plea of ill-health was only met by smiles from the young ladies, and the reply that a ride would effect a cure.

Dressed in a scarlet coat and high boots, with the low, round cap worn in the chase, Jerome mounted a high-spirited horse, whip in hand, and made himself one of the party. In America, riding is a necessity; in England, it is a pleasure. Young men and women attend riding-school in our fatherland, and consider that they are studying a science. Jerome was no rider. He had not been on horseback for more than ten years, and as soon as he mounted, every one saw that he was a novice, and a smile was on the countenance of each member of the company.

The blowing of the horn, and assembling of the hounds, and finally the release of the fox from his close prison, were the signals for the chase to commence. The first half-mile the little animal took his course over a beautiful field where there was neither hedge nor ditch. Thus far the chase was enjoyed by all, even by the American rider, who was better fitted to witness the scene than to take part in it.

We left Jerome in our last reluctantly engaged in the chase; and though the first mile or so of the pursuit, which was over smooth meadow-land, had had an exhilarating effect upon his mind, and tended somewhat to relieve him of the embarrassment consequent upon his position, he nevertheless still felt that he was far from being in his proper element. Besides, the fox had now made for a dense forest which lay before, and he saw difficulties in that direction which to him appeared insurmountable.

Away went the huntsmen, over stone walls, high fences, and deep ditches. Jerome saw the ladies even leading the gentlemen, but this could not inspire him. They cleared the fences, four and five feet high with perfect ease, showing they were quite at home in the saddle. But alas for the poor American! As his fine steed came up to the first fence, and was about to make the leap, Jerome pulled at the bridle, and cried at the top of his voice, "Whoa! whoa! whoa!" the horse at the same time capering about, and appearing determined to keep up with the other animals.

Away dashed the huntsmen, following the hounds, and all were soon lost to the view of their colored companion. Jerome rode up and down the field looking for a gate or bars, that he might get through without risking his neck. Finding, however, that all hope of again catching up with the party was out of the question, he determined to return to the house, under a plea of sudden illness, and back he accordingly went.

"I hope no accident has happened to your honor," said the groom, as he met our hero at the gate.

"A slight dizziness," was the answer.

One of the servants, without being ordered, went at once for the family physician. Ashamed to own that his return was owing to his inability to ride, Jerome resolved to feign sickness. The doctor came, felt his pulse, examined his tongue, and pronounced him a sick man. He immediately ordered a tepid bath, and sent for a couple of leeches.

Seeing things taking such a serious turn, the American began to regret the part he was playing; for there was no fun in being rubbed and leeched when one was in perfect health. He had gone too far to recede, however, and so submitted quietly to the directions of the doctor; and, after following the injunctions given by that learned Esculapius, was put to bed.

Shortly after, the sound of the horns and the yelp of the hounds announced that the poor fox had taken the back track, and was repassing near the house. Even the pleasure of witnessing the beautiful sight from the window was denied to our hero; for the physician had ordered that he must be kept in perfect quiet.

The chase was at last over, and the huntsmen all in, sympathizing with their lost companion. After nine days of sweating, blistering and leeching, Jerome left his bed convalescent, but much reduced in flesh and strength. This was his first and last attempt to follow the fox and hounds.

During his fortnight's stay at Colonel G.'s, Jerome spent most of his time in the magnificent library. Claude did not watch with more interest every color of the skies, the trees, the grass, and the water, to learn from nature, than did this son of a despised race search books to obtain that knowledge which his early life as a slave had denied him.

CHAPTER XXXI
THE MYSTERIOUS MEETING.

After more than a fortnight spent in the highlands of Scotland, Jerome passed hastily through London on his way to the continent.

It was toward sunset, on a warm day in October, shortly after his arrival in France, that, after strolling some distance from the Hotel de Leon, in the old and picturesque town of Dunkirk, he entered a burial ground--such places being always favorite walks with him--and wandered around among the silent dead. All nature around was hushed in silence, and seemed to partake of the general melancholy that hung over the quiet resting-place of the departed. Even the birds seemed imbued with the spirit of the place, for they were silent, either flying noiselessly over the graves, or jumping about in the tall grass. After tracing the various inscriptions that told the characters and conditions of the deceased, and viewing the mounds beneath which the dust of mortality slumbered, he arrived at a secluded spot near where an aged weeping willow bowed its thick foliage to the ground, as though anxious to hide from the scrutinizing gaze of curiosity the grave beneath it. Jerome seated himself on a marble tombstone, and commenced reading from a book which he had carried under his arm. It was now twilight, and he had read but a few minutes when he observed a lady, attired in deep black, and leading a boy, apparently some five or six years old, coming up one of the beautiful, winding paths. As the lady's veil was drawn closely over her face, he felt somewhat at liberty to eye her more closely. While thus engaged, the lady gave a slight scream, and seemed suddenly to have fallen into a fainting condition. Jerome sprang from his seat, and caught her in time to save her from falling to the ground.

At this moment an elderly gentleman, also dressed in black, was seen approaching with a hurried step, which seemed to indicate that he was in some way connected with the lady. The old man came up, and in rather a confused manner inquired what had happened, and Jerome explained matters as well as he was able to do so. After taking up the vinaigrette, which had fallen from her hand, and holding the bottle a short time to her face, the lady began to revive. During all this time, the veil had still partly covered the face of the fair one, so that Jerome had scarcely seen it. When she had so far recovered as to be able to look around her, she raised herself slightly, and again screamed and swooned. The old man now feeling satisfied that Jerome's dark complexion was the immediate cause of the catastrophe, said in a somewhat petulant tone,--

"I will be glad, sir, if you will leave us alone."

The little boy at this juncture set up a loud cry, and amid the general confusion, Jerome left the ground and returned to his hotel.

While seated at the window of his room looking out upon the crowded street, with every now and then the strange scene in the graveyard vividly before him, Jerome suddenly thought of the book he had been reading, and, remembering that he had left it on the tombstone, where he dropped it when called to the lady's assistance, he determined to return for it at once.

After a walk of some twenty minutes, he found himself again in the burial-ground and on the spot where he had been an hour before. The pensive moon was already up, and its soft light was sleeping on the little pond at the back of the grounds, while the stars seemed smiling at their own sparkling rays gleaming up from the beautiful sheet of water.

Jerome searched in vain for his book; it was nowhere to be found. Nothing, save the bouquet that the lady had dropped and which lay half-buried in the grass, from having been trodden upon, indicated that any one had been there that evening. The stillness of death reigned over the place; even the little birds, that had before been twittering and flying about, had retired for the night.

Taking up the bunch of flowers, Jerome returned to his hotel.

"What can this mean?" he would ask himself; "and why should they take my book?" These questions he put to himself again and again during his walk. His sleep was broken more than once that night, and he welcomed the early dawn as it made its appearance.

CHAPTER XXXII
THE HAPPY MEETING.

After passing a sleepless night, and hearing the clock strike six, Jerome took from his table a book, and thus endeavored to pass away the hours before breakfast-time. While thus engaged, a servant entered and handed him a note. Hastily tearing it open, Jerome read as follows:--

"Sir,--I owe you an apology for the abrupt manner in which I addressed you last evening, and the inconvenience to which you were subjected by some of my household. If you will honor us with your presence to-day at four o'clock, I shall be most happy to give you due satisfaction. My servant will be waiting with the carriage at half-past three.

I am, sir, yours, &c,
J. DEVENANT.   JEROME FLETCHER, Esq."

Who this gentleman was, and how he had found out his name and the hotel at which he was stopping, were alike mysteries to Jerome. And this note seemed to his puzzled brain like a challenge. "Satisfaction?" He had not asked for satisfaction. However, he resolved to accept the invitation, and, if need be, meet the worst. At any rate, this most mysterious and complicated affair would be explained.

The clock on a neighboring church had scarcely finished striking three when a servant announced to Jerome that a carriage had called for him. In a few minutes, he was seated in a sumptuous barouche, drawn by a pair of beautiful iron-grays, and rolling over a splendid gravel road entirely shaded by trees, which appeared to have been the accumulated growth of many centuries. The carriage soon stopped at a low villa, which was completely embowered in trees.

Jerome alighted, and was shown into a superb room, with the walls finely decorated with splendid tapestry, and the ceilings exquisitely frescoed. The walls were hung with fine specimens from the hands of the great Italian masters, and one by a German artist, representing a beautiful monkish legend connected with the "Holy Catharine," an illustrious lady of Alexandria. High-backed chairs stood around the room, rich curtains of crimson damask hung in folds on either side of the window, and a beautiful, rich, Turkey carpet covered the floor. In the centre of the room stood a table covered with books, in the midst of which was a vase of fresh flowers, loading the atmosphere with their odors. A faint light, together with the quiet of the hour, gave beauty beyond description to the whole scene. A half-open door showed a fine marble floor to an adjoining room, with pictures, statues, and antiquated sofas, and flower-pots filled with rare plants of every kind and description.

Jerome had scarcely run his eyes over the beauties of the room when the elderly gentleman whom he had met on the previous evening made his appearance, followed by the little boy, and introduced himself as Mr. Devenant. A moment more and a lady, a beautiful brunette, dressed in black, with long black curls hanging over her shoulders, entered the room. Her dark, bright eyes flashed as she caught the first sight of Jerome. The gentleman immediately arose on the entrance of the lady, and Mr. Devenant was in the act of introducing the stranger when he observed that Jerome had sunk back upon the sofa, in a faint voice exclaiming,--

"It is she!"

After this, all was dark and dreary. How long he remained in this condition, it was for others to tell. The lady knelt by his side and wept; and when he came to, he found himself stretched upon the sofa with his boots off and his head resting upon a pillow. By his side sat the old man, with the smelling-bottle in one hand and a glass of water in the other, while the little boy stood at the foot of the sofa. As soon as Jerome had so far recovered as to be able to speak, he said,--

"Where am I, and what does all this mean?"

"Wait awhile," replied the old man, "and I will tell you all."

After the lapse of some ten minutes, Jerome arose from the sofa, adjusted his apparel, and said,--

"I am now ready to hear anything you have to say."

"You were born in America?" said the old man.

"I was," he replied.

"And you knew a girl named Clotelle," continued the old man.

"Yes, and I loved her as I can love none other."

"The lady whom you met so mysteriously last evening was she," said Mr. Devenant.

Jerome was silent, but the fountain of mingled grief and joy stole out from beneath his eyelashes, and glistened like pearls upon his ebony cheeks.

At this juncture, the lady again entered the room. With an enthusiasm that can be better imagined than described, Jerome sprang from the sofa, and they rushed into each other's arms, to the great surprise of the old gentleman and little Autoine, and to the amusement of the servants who had crept up, one by one and were hid behind the doors or loitering in the hall. When they had given vent to their feelings and sufficiently recovered their presence of mind, they resumed their seats.

"How did you find out my name and address?" inquired Jerome.

"After you had left the grave-yard," replied Clotelle, "our little boy said, 'Oh, mamma! if there ain't a book!' I opened the book, and saw your name written in it, and also found a card of the Hotel de Leon. Papa wished to leave the book, and said it was only a fancy of mine that I had ever seen you before; but I was perfectly convinced that you were my own dear Jerome."

As she uttered the last words, tears--the sweet bright tears that love alone can bring forth--bedewed her cheeks.

"Are you married?" now inquired Clotelle, with a palpitating heart and trembling voice.

"No, I am not, and never have been," was Jerome's reply.

"Then, thank God!" she exclaimed, in broken accents.

It was then that hope gleamed up amid the crushed and broken flowers of her heart, and a bright flash darted forth like a sunbeam.

"Are you single now?" asked Jerome.

"Yes, I am," was the answer.

"Then you will be mine after all?" said he with a smile.

Her dark, rich hair had partly come down, and hung still more loosely over her shoulders than when she first appeared; and her eyes, now full of animation and vivacity, and her sweet, harmonious, and well-modulated voice, together with her modesty, self-possession, and engaging manners, made Clotelle appear lovely beyond description. Although past the age when men ought to think of matrimony, yet the scene before Mr. Devenant brought vividly to his mind the time when he was young and had a loving bosom companion living, and tears were wiped from the old man's eyes. A new world seemed to unfold itself before the eyes of the happy lovers, and they were completely absorbed in contemplating the future. Furnished by nature with a disposition to study, and a memory so retentive that all who knew her were surprised at the ease with which she acquired her education and general information, Clotelle might now be termed a most accomplished lady. After her marriage with young Devenant, they proceeded to India, where the husband's regiment was stationed. Soon after their arrival, however, a battle was fought with the natives, in which several officers fell, among whom was Captain Devenant. The father of the young captain being there at the time, took his daughter-in-law and brought her back to France, where they took up their abode at the old homestead.

Old Mr. Devenant was possessed of a large fortune, all of which he intended for his daughter-in-law and her only child.

Although Clotelle had married young Devenant, she had not forgotten her first love, and her father-in-law now willingly gave his consent to her marriage with Jerome. Jerome felt that to possess the woman of his love, even at that late hour, was compensation enough for the years that he had been separated from her, and Clotelle wanted no better evidence of his love for her than the fact of his having remained so long unmarried. It was indeed a rare instance of devotion and constancy in a man, and the young widow gratefully appreciated it.

It was late in the evening when Jerome led his intended bride to the window, and the magnificent moonlight illuminated the countenance of the lovely Clotelle, while inward sunshine, emanating from a mind at ease, and her own virtuous thoughts, gave brightness to her eyes and made her appear a very angel. This was the first evening that Jerome had been in her company since the night when, to effect his escape from prison, she disguised herself in male attire. How different the scene now. Free instead of slaves, wealthy instead of poor, and on the eve of an event that seemed likely to result in a life of happiness to both.

CHAPTER XXXIII
THE HAPPY DAY.

It was a bright day in the latter part of October that Jerome and Clotelle set out for the church, where the marriage ceremony was to be performed. The clear, bracing air added buoyancy to every movement, and the sun poured its brilliant rays through the deeply-stained windows, as the happy couple entered the sanctuary, followed by old Mr. Devenant, whose form, bowed down with age, attracted almost as much attention from the assembly as did the couple more particularly interested.

As the ceremonies were finished and the priest pronounced the benediction on the newly-married pair, Clotelle whispered in the ear of Jerome,--

"'No power in death shall tear our names apart, As none in life could rend thee from my heart.'"

A smile beamed on every face as the wedding-party left the church and entered their carriage. What a happy day, after ten years' separation, when, both hearts having been blighted for a time, they are brought together by the hand of a beneficent and kind Providence, and united in holy wedlock.

Everything being arranged for a wedding tour extending up the Rhine, the party set out the same day for Antwerp. There are many rivers of greater length and width than the Rhine. Our Mississippi would swallow up half a dozen Rhines. The Hudson is grander, the Tiber, the Po, and the Minclo more classic; the Thames and

Seine bear upon their waters greater amounts of wealth and commerce; the Nile and the Euphrates have a greater antiquity; but for a combination of interesting historical incidents and natural scenery, the Rhine surpasses them all. Nature has so ordained it that those who travel in the valley of the Rhine shall see the river, for there never will be a railroad upon its banks. So mountainous is the land that it would have to be one series of tunnels. Every three or four miles from the time you enter this glorious river, hills, dales, castles, and crags present themselves as the steamer glides onward.

Their first resting-place for any length of time was at Coblentz, at the mouth of the "Blue Moselle," the most interesting place on the river. From Coblentz they went to Brussels, where they had the greatest attention paid them. Besides being provided with letters of introduction, Jerome's complexion secured for him more deference than is usually awarded to travellers.

Having letters of introduction to M. Deceptiax, the great lace manufacturer, that gentleman received them with distinguished honors, and gave them a splendid soiree, at which the elite of the city were assembled. The sumptuously-furnished mansion was lavishly decorated for the occasion, and every preparation made that could add to the novelty or interest of the event.

Jerome, with his beautiful bride, next visited Cologne, the largest and wealthiest city on the banks of the Rhine. The Cathedral of Cologne is the most splendid structure of the kind in Europe, and Jerome and Clotelle viewed with interest the beautiful arches and columns of this stupendous building, which strikes with awe the beholder, as he gazes at its unequalled splendor, surrounded, as it is, by villas, cottages, and palace-like mansions, with the enchanting Rhine winding through the vine-covered hills.

After strolling over miles and miles of classic ground, and visiting castles, whose legends and traditions have given them an enduring fame, our delighted travellers started for Geneva, bidding the picturesque banks of the Rhine a regretful farewell. Being much interested in literature, and aware that Geneva was noted for having been the city of refuge to the victims of religious and political persecution, Jerome arranged to stay here for some days. He was provided with a letter of introduction to M. de Stee, who had been a fellow-soldier of Mr. Devenant in the East India wars, and they were invited to make his house their home during their sojourn. On the side of a noble mountain, whose base is kissed by the waves of Lake Geneva, and whose slopes are decked with verdure to the utmost peak of its rocky crown, is situated the delightful country residence of this wealthy, retired French officer. A winding road, with frequent climbs and brakes, leads from the valley to this enchanting spot, the air and scenery of which cannot be surpassed in the world.

CHAPTER XXXIV
CLOTELLE MEETS HER FATHER.

The clouds that had skirted the sky during the day broke at last, and the rain fell in torrents, as Jerome and Clotelle retired for the night, in the little town of Ferney, on the borders of Lake Leman. The peals of thunder, and flashes of vivid lightening, which seemed to leap from mountain to mountain and from crag to crag, reverberating among the surrounding hills, foretold a heavy storm.

"I would we were back at Geneva," said Clotelle, as she heard groans issuing from an adjoining room. The sounds, at first faint, grew louder and louder, plainly indicating that some person was suffering extreme pain.

"I did not like this hotel, much, when we came in," I said Jerome, relighting the lamp, which had been accidentally extinguished.

"Nor I," returned Clotelle.

The shrieks increased, and an occasional "She's dead!" "I killed her!" "No, she is not dead!" and such-like expressions, would be heard from the person, who seemed to be deranged.

The thunder grew louder, and the flashes of lightning more vivid, while the noise from the sick-room seemed to increase.

As Jerome opened the door, to learn, if possible, the cause of the cries and groans, he could distinguish the words, "She's dead! yes, she's dead! but I did not kill her. She was my child! my own daughter. I loved her, and yet I did not protect her."

"Whoever he is," said Jerome, "he's crack-brained; some robber, probably, from the mountains."

The storm continued to rage, and the loud peals of thunder and sharp flashes of lightening, together with the shrieks and moans of the maniac in the adjoining room, made the night a fearful one. The long hours wore slowly away, but neither Jerome nor his wife could sleep, and they arose at an early hour in the morning, ordered breakfast, and resolved to return to Geneva.

"I am sorry, sir, that you were so much disturbed by the sick man last night," said the landlord, as he handed Jerome his bill. "I should be glad if he would get able to go away, or die, for he's a deal of trouble to me. Several persons have left my house on his account."

"Where is he from?" inquired Jerome.

"He's from the United States, and has been here a week to-day, and has been crazy ever since."

"Has he no friends with him?" asked the guest.

"No, he is alone," was the reply.

Jerome related to his wife what he had learned from the landlord, respecting the sick man, and the intelligence impressed her so strongly, that she requested him to make further inquiries concerning the stranger.

He therefore consulted the book in which guests usually register their names, and, to his great surprise, found that the American's name was Henry Linwood, and that he was from Richmond, Va.

It was with feelings of trepidation that Clotelle heard these particulars from the lips of her husband.

"We must see this poor man, whoever he is," said she, as Jerome finished the sentence.

The landlord was glad to hear that his guests felt some interest in the sick man, and promised that the invalid's room should be got ready for their reception.

The clock in the hall was just striking ten, as Jerome passed through and entered the sick man's chamber. Stretched upon a mattress, with both hands tightly bound to the bedstead, the friendless stranger was indeed a pitiful sight. His dark, dishevelled hair prematurely gray, his long, unshaven beard, and the wildness of the eyes which glanced upon them as they opened the door and entered, caused the faint hope which had so suddenly risen in Clotelle's heart, to sink, and she felt that this man could claim no kindred with her. Certainly, he bore no resemblance to the man whom she had called her father, and who had fondly dandled her on his knee in those happy days of childhood.

"Help!" cried the poor man, as Jerome and his wife walked into the room. His eyes glared, and shriek after shriek broke forth from his parched and fevered lips.

"No, I did not kill my daughter!--I did not! she is not dead! Yes, she is dead! but I did not kill her--poor girl Look! that is she! No, it cannot be! she cannot come here! it cannot be my poor Clotelle."

At the sound of her own name, coming from the maniac's lips, Clotelle gasped for breath, and her husband saw that she had grown deadly pale. It seemed evident to him that the man was either guilty of some terrible act, or imagined himself to be. His eyeballs rolled in their sockets, and his features showed that he was undergoing "the tortures of that inward hell," which seemed to set his whole brain on fire.

After recovering her self-possession and strength, Clotelle approached the bedside, and laid her soft hand upon the stranger's hot and fevered brow.

One long, loud shriek rang out on the air, and a piercing cry, "It is she!---Yes, it is she! I see, I see! Ah! no, it is not my daughter! She would not come to me if she could!" broke forth from him.

"I am your daughter," said Clotelle, as she pressed her handkerchief to her face, and sobbed aloud.

Like balls of fire, the poor man's eyes rolled and glared upon the company, while large drops of perspiration ran down his pale and emaciated face. Strange as the scene appeared, all present saw that it was indeed a meeting between a father and his long-lost daughter. Jerome now ordered all present to leave the room, except the nurse, and every effort was at once made to quiet the sufferer. When calm, a joyous smile would illuminate the sick man's face, and a strange light beam in his eyes, as he seemed to realize that she who stood before him was indeed his child.

For two long days and nights did Clotelle watch at the bedside of her father before he could speak to her intelligently. Sometimes, in his insane fits, he would rave in the most frightful manner, and then, in a few moments, would be as easily governed as a child. At last, however, after a long and apparently refreshing sleep, he awoke suddenly to a full consciousness that it was indeed his daughter who was watching so patiently by his side.

The presence of his long absent child had a soothing effect upon Mr. Linwood, and he now recovered rapidly from the sad and almost hopeless condition in which she had found him. When able to converse, without danger of a relapse, he told Clotelle of his fruitless efforts to obtain a clew to her whereabouts after old Mrs. Miller had sold her to the slave-trader. In answer to his daughter's inquiries about his family affairs up to the time that he left America, he said,--

"I blamed my wife for your being sold and sent away, for I thought she and her mother were acting in collusion; But I afterwards found that I had blamed her wrongfully. Poor woman! she knew that I loved your mother, and feeling herself forsaken, she grew melancholy and died in a decline three years ago."

Here both father and daughter wept at the thought of other days. When they had recovered their composure, Mr. Linwood went on again:

"Old Mrs. Miller," said he, "after the death of Gertrude, aware that she had contributed much toward her unhappiness, took to the free use of intoxicating drinks, and became the most brutal creature that ever lived. She whipped her slaves without the slightest provocation, and seemed to take delight in inventing new tortures with which to punish them. One night last winter, after having flogged one of her slaves nearly to death, she returned to her room, and by some means the bedding took fire, and the house was in flames before any one was awakened. There was no one in the building at the time but the old woman and the slaves, and although the latter might have saved their mistress, they made no attempt to do so. Thus, after a frightful career of many years, this hard-hearted woman died a most miserable death, unlamented by a single person."

Clotelle wiped the tears from her eyes, as her father finished this story, for, although Mrs. Miller had been her greatest enemy, she regretted to learn that her end had been such a sad one.

"My peace of mind destroyed," resumed the father, "and broke down in health, my physician advised me to travel, with the hope o recruiting myself, and I sailed from New York two months ago."

Being brought up in America, and having all the prejudice against color which characterizes his white fellow-countrymen, Mr. Linwood very much regretted that his daughter, although herself tinctured with African blood, should have married a black man, and he did not fail to express to her his dislike of her husband's complexion.

"I married him," said Clotelle, "because I loved him. Why should the white man be esteemed as better than the black? I find no difference in men on account of their complexion. One of the cardinal principles of Christianity and freedom is the equality and brotherhood of man."

Every day Mr. Linwood became more and more familiar with Jerome, and eventually they were on the most intimate terms.

Fifteen days from the time that Clotelle was introduced into her father's room, they left Ferney for Geneva. Many were the excursions Clotelle made under the shadows of Mont Blanc, and with her husband and father for companions; she was now in the enjoyment of pleasures hitherto unknown.

CHAPTER XXXV
THE FATHER'S RESOLVE.

Aware that her father was still a slave-owner, Clotelle determined to use all her persuasive power to induce him to set them free, and in this effort she found a substantial supporter in her husband.

"I have always treated my slaves well," said Mr. Linwood to Jerome, as the latter expressed his abhorrence of the system; "and my neighbors, too, are generally good men; for slavery in. Virginia is not like slavery in the other States," continued the proud son of the Old Dominion.

"Their right to be free, Mr. Linwood," said Jerome, "is taken from them, and they have no security for their comfort, but the humanity and generosity of men, who have been trained to regard them not as brethren, but as mere property. Humanity and generosity are, at best, but poor guaranties for the protection of those who cannot assert their rights, and over whom law throws no protection."

It was with pleasure that Clotelle obtained from her father a promise that he would liberate all his slaves on his return to Richmond. In a beautiful little villa, situated in a pleasant spot, fringed with hoary rocks and thick dark woods, within sight of the deep blue waters of Lake Leman, Mr. Linwood, his daughter, and her husband, took up their residence for a short time. For more than three weeks, this little party spent their time in visiting the birth-place of Rousseau, and the former abodes of Byron, Gibbon, Voltaire, De Stael, Shelley, and other literary characters.

We can scarcely contemplate a visit to a more historic and interesting place than Geneva and its vicinity. Here, Calvin, that great luminary in the Church, lived and ruled for years; here, Voltaire, the mighty genius, who laid the foundation of the French Revolution, and who boasted, "When I shake my wig, I powder the whole republic," governed in the higher walks of life.

Fame is generally the recompense, not of the living, but of the dead,--not always do they reap and gather in the harvest who sow the seed; the flame of its altar is too often kindled from the ashes of the great. A distinguished critic has beautifully said, "The sound which the stream of high thought, carried down to future ages, makes, as it flows--deep, distant, murmuring ever more, like the waters of the mighty ocean." No reputation can be called great that will not endure this test. The distinguished men who had lived in Geneva transfused their spirit, by their writings, into the spirit of other lovers of literature and everything that treated of great authors. Jerome and Clotelle lingered long in and about the haunts of Geneva and Lake Leman.

An autumn sun sent down her bright rays, and bathed every object in her glorious light, as Clotelle, accompanied by her husband and father set out one fine morning on her return home to France. Throughout the whole route, Mr. Linwood saw by the deference paid to Jerome, whose black complexion excited astonishment in those who met him, that there was no hatred to the man in Europe, on account of his color; that what is called prejudice against color is the offspring of the institution of slavery; and he felt ashamed of his own countrymen, when he thought of the complexion as distinctions, made in the United States, and resolved to dedicate the remainder of his life to the eradication of this unrepublican and unchristian feeling from the land of his birth, on his return home.

After a stay of four weeks at Dunkirk, the home of the Fletchers, Mr. Linwood set out for America, with the full determination of freeing his slaves, and settling them in one of the Northern States, and then to return to France to end his days in the society of his beloved daughter.

THE END.

NOTE.--The author of the foregoing tale was formerly a Kentucky slave. If it serves to relieve the monotony of camp-life to the soldiers of the Union, and therefore of Liberty, and at the same time kindles their zeal in the cause of universal emancipation, the object both of its author and publisher will be gained. J. R.

The Codes Of Hammurabi And Moses
W. W. Davies

QTY

The discovery of the Hammurabi Code is one of the greatest achievements of archaeology, and is of paramount interest, not only to the student of the Bible, but also to all those interested in ancient history...

Religion   ISBN: *1-59462-338-4*

Pages:132
MSRP $12.95

The Theory of Moral Sentiments
Adam Smith

QTY

This work from 1749. contains original theories of conscience amd moral judgment and it is the foundation for systemof morals.

Philosophy ISBN: *1-59462-777-0*

Pages:536
MSRP $19.95

Jessica's First Prayer
Hesba Stretton

QTY

In a screened and secluded corner of one of the many railway-bridges which span the streets of London there could be seen a few years ago, from five o'clock every morning until half past eight, a tidily set-out coffee-stall, consisting of a trestle and board, upon which stood two large tin cans, with a small fire of charcoal burning under each so as to keep the coffee boiling during the early hours of the morning when the work-people were thronging into the city on their way to their daily toil...

Childrens   ISBN: *1-59462-373-2*

Pages:84
MSRP $9.95

My Life and Work
Henry Ford

QTY

Henry Ford revolutionized the world with his implementation of mass production for the Model T automobile. Gain valuable business insight into his life and work with his own auto-biography... "We have only started on our development of our country we have not as yet, with all our talk of wonderful progress, done more than scratch the surface. The progress has been wonderful enough but..."

Biographies/   ISBN: *1-59462-198-5*

Pages:300
MSRP $21.95

The Art of Cross-Examination
Francis Wellman

QTY

I presume it is the experience of every author, after his first book is published upon an important subject, to be almost overwhelmed with a wealth of ideas and illustrations which could readily have been included in his book, and which to his own mind, at least, seem to make a second edition inevitable. Such certainly was the case with me; and when the first edition had reached its sixth impression in five months, I rejoiced to learn that it seemed to my publishers that the book had met with a sufficiently favorable reception to justify a second and considerably enlarged edition. ..

Reference   **ISBN: *1-59462-647-2***

Pages:412

MSRP $19.95

On the Duty of Civil Disobedience
Henry David Thoreau

QTY

Thoreau wrote his famous essay, On the Duty of Civil Disobedience, as a protest against an unjust but popular war and the immoral but popular institution of slave-owning. He did more than write—he declined to pay his taxes, and was hauled off to gaol in consequence. Who can say how much this refusal of his hastened the end of the war and of slavery ?

Law   **ISBN: *1-59462-747-9***

Pages:48

MSRP $7.45

Dream Psychology Psychoanalysis for Beginners
Sigmund Freud

QTY

Sigmund Freud, born Sigismund Schlomo Freud (May 6, 1856 - September 23, 1939), was a Jewish-Austrian neurologist and psychiatrist who co-founded the psychoanalytic school of psychology. Freud is best known for his theories of the unconscious mind, especially involving the mechanism of repression; his redefinition of sexual desire as mobile and directed towards a wide variety of objects; and his therapeutic techniques, especially his understanding of transference in the therapeutic relationship and the presumed value of dreams as sources of insight into unconscious desires.

Psychology   **ISBN: *1-59462-905-6***

Pages:196

MSRP $15.45

The Miracle of Right Thought
Orison Swett Marden

QTY

Believe with all of your heart that you will do what you were made to do. When the mind has once formed the habit of holding cheerful, happy, prosperous pictures, it will not be easy to form the opposite habit. It does not matter how improbable or how far away this realization may see, or how dark the prospects may be, if we visualize them as best we can, as vividly as possible, hold tenaciously to them and vigorously struggle to attain them, they will gradually become actualized, realized in the life. But a desire, a longing without endeavor, a yearning abandoned or held indifferently will vanish without realization.

Pages:360

Self Help   **ISBN: *1-59462-644-8***

MSRP $25.45

The Rosicrucian Cosmo-Conception Mystic Christianity *by Max Heindel*   ISBN: 1-59462-188-8   **$38.95**
The Rosicrucian Cosmo-conception is not dogmatic, neither does it appeal to any other authority than the reason of the student. It is; not controversial, but is: sent forth in the, hope that it may help to clear...   New Age/Religion Pages 646

Abandonment To Divine Providence *by Jean-Pierre de Caussade*   ISBN: 1-59462-228-0   **$25.95**
"The Rev. Jean Pierre de Caussade was one of the most remarkable spiritual writers of the Society of Jesus in France in the 18th Century. His death took place at Toulouse in 1751. His works have gone through many editions and have been republished...   Inspirational/Religion Pages 400

Mental Chemistry *by Charles Haanel*   ISBN: 1-59462-192-6   **$23.95**
Mental Chemistry allows the change of material conditions by combining and appropriately utilizing the power of the mind. Much like applied chemistry creates something new and unique out of careful combinations of chemicals the mastery of mental chemistry...   New Age Pages 354

The Letters of Robert Browning and Elizabeth Barret Barrett 1845-1846 vol II   ISBN: 1-59462-193-4   **$35.95**
by Robert Browning and Elizabeth Barrett   Biographies Pages 596

Gleanings In Genesis (volume I) *by Arthur W. Pink*   ISBN: 1-59462-130-6   **$27.45**
Appropriately has Genesis been termed "the seed plot of the Bible" for in it we have, in germ form, almost all of the great doctrines which are afterwards fully developed in the books of Scripture which follow...   Religion/Inspirational Pages 420

The Master Key *by L. W. de Laurence*   ISBN: 1-59462-001-6   **$30.95**
In no branch of human knowledge has there been a more lively increase of the spirit of research during the past few years than in the study of Psychology, Concentration and Mental Discipline. The requests for authentic lessons in Thought Control, Mental Discipline and...   New Age/Business Pages 422

The Lesser Key Of Solomon Goetia *by L. W. de Laurence*   ISBN: 1-59462-092-X   **$9.95**
This translation of the first book of the "Lernegton" which is now for the first time made accessible to students of Talismanic Magic was done, after careful collation and edition, from numerous Ancient Manuscripts in Hebrew, Latin, and French...   New Age/Occult Pages 92

Rubaiyat Of Omar Khayyam *by Edward Fitzgerald*   ISBN:1-59462-332-5   **$13.95**
Edward Fitzgerald, whom the world has already learned, in spite of his own efforts to remain within the shadow of anonymity, to look upon as one of the rarest poets of the century, was born at Bredfield, in Suffolk, on the 31st of March, 1809. He was the third son of John Purcell...   Music Pages 172

Ancient Law *by Henry Maine*   ISBN: 1-59462-128-4   **$29.95**
The chief object of the following pages is to indicate some of the earliest ideas of mankind, as they are reflected in Ancient Law, and to point out the relation of those ideas to modern thought.   Religiom/History Pages 452

Far-Away Stories *by William J. Locke*   ISBN: 1-59462-129-2   **$19.45**
"Good wine needs no bush, but a collection of mixed vintages does. And this book is just such a collection. Some of the stories I do not want to remain buried for ever in the museum files of dead magazine-numbers an author's not unpardonable vanity..."   Fiction Pages 272

Life of David Crockett *by David Crockett*   ISBN: 1-59462-250-7   **$27.45**
"Colonel David Crockett was one of the most remarkable men of the times in which he lived. Born in humble life, but gifted with a strong will, an indomitable courage, and unremitting perseverance...   Biographies/New Age Pages 424

Lip-Reading *by Edward Nitchie*   ISBN: 1-59462-206-X   **$25.95**
Edward B. Nitchie, founder of the New York School for the Hard of Hearing, now the Nitchie School of Lip-Reading, Inc, wrote "LIP-READING Principles and Practice". The development and perfecting of this meritorious work on lip-reading was an undertaking...   How-to Pages 400

A Handbook of Suggestive Therapeutics, Applied Hypnotism, Psychic Science   ISBN: 1-59462-214-0   **$24.95**
by Henry Munro   Health/New Age/Health/Self-help Pages 376

A Doll's House: and Two Other Plays *by Henrik Ibsen*   ISBN: 1-59462-112-8   **$19.95**
Henrik Ibsen created this classic when in revolutionary 1848 Rome. Introducing some striking concepts in playwriting for the realist genre, this play has been studied the world over.   Fiction/Classics/Plays 308

The Light of Asia *by sir Edwin Arnold*   ISBN: 1-59462-204-3   **$13.95**
In this poetic masterpiece, Edwin Arnold describes the life and teachings of Buddha. The man who was to become known as Buddha to the world was born as Prince Gautama of India but he rejected the worldly riches and abandoned the reigns of power when...   Religion/History/Biographies Pages 170

The Complete Works of Guy de Maupassant *by Guy de Maupassant*   ISBN: 1-59462-157-8   **$16.95**
"For days and days, nights and nights, I had dreamed of that first kiss which was to consecrate our engagement, and I knew not on what spot I should put my lips..."   Fiction/Classics Pages 240

The Art of Cross-Examination *by Francis L. Wellman*   ISBN: 1-59462-309-0   **$26.95**
Written by a renowned trial lawyer, Wellman imparts his experience and uses case studies to explain how to use psychology to extract desired information through questioning.   How-to/Science/Reference Pages 408

Answered or Unanswered? *by Louisa Vaughan*   ISBN: 1-59462-248-5   **$10.95**
Miracles of Faith in China   Religion Pages 112

The Edinburgh Lectures on Mental Science (1909) *by Thomas*   ISBN: 1-59462-008-3   **$11.95**
This book contains the substance of a course of lectures recently given by the writer in the Queen Street Hall, Edinburgh. Its purpose is to indicate the Natural Principles governing the relation between Mental Action and Material Conditions...   New Age/Psychology Pages 148

Ayesha *by H. Rider Haggard*   ISBN: 1-59462-301-5   **$24.95**
Verily and indeed it is the unexpected that happens! Probably if there was one person upon the earth from whom the Editor of this, and of a certain previous history, did not expect to hear again...   Classics Pages 380

Ayala's Angel *by Anthony Trollope*   ISBN: 1-59462-352-X   **$29.95**
The two girls were both pretty, but Lucy who was twenty-one who supposed to be simple and comparatively unattractive, whereas Ayala was credited, as her Bombwhat romantic name might show, with poetic charm and a taste for romance. Ayala when her father died was nineteen...   Fiction Pages 484

The American Commonwealth *by James Bryce*   ISBN: 1-59462-286-8   **$34.45**
An interpretation of American democratic political theory. It examines political mechanics and society from the perspective of Scotsman James Bryce   Politics Pages 572

Stories of the Pilgrims *by Margaret P. Pumphrey*   ISBN: 1-59462-116-0   **$17.95**
This book explores pilgrims religious oppression in England as well as their escape to Holland and eventual crossing to America on the Mayflower, and their early days in New England...   History Pages 268

www.bookjungle.com *email: sales@bookjungle.com fax: 630-214-0564 mail: Book Jungle PO Box 2226 Champaign, IL 61825*

QTY

The Fasting Cure *by Sinclair Upton* ISBN: *1-59462-222-1* $13.95
In the Cosmopolitan Magazine for May, 1910, and in the Contemporary Review (London) for April, 1910, I published an article dealing with my experiences in fasting. I have written a great many magazine articles, but never one which attracted so much attention... New Age/Self Help/Health Pages 164

Hebrew Astrology *by Sepharial* ISBN: *1-59462-308-2* $13.45
In these days of advanced thinking it is a matter of common observation that we have left many of the old landmarks behind and that we are now pressing forward to greater heights and to a wider horizon than that which represented the mind-content of our progenitors... Astrology Pages 144

Thought Vibration or The Law of Attraction in the Thought World ISBN: *1-59462-127-6* $12.95
by William Walker Atkinson Psychology/Religion Pages 144

Optimism *by Helen Keller* ISBN: *1-59462-108-X* $15.95
Helen Keller was blind, deaf, and mute since 19 months old, yet famously learned how to overcome these handicaps, communicate with the world, and spread her lectures promoting optimism. An inspiring read for everyone... Biographies/Inspirational Pages 84

Sara Crewe *by Frances Burnett* ISBN: *1-59462-360-0* $9.45
In the first place, Miss Minchin lived in London. Her home was a large, dull, tall one, in a large, dull square, where all the houses were alike, and all the sparrows were alike, and where all the door-knockers made the same heavy sound... Childrens/Classic Pages 88

The Autobiography of Benjamin Franklin *by Benjamin Franklin* ISBN: *1-59462-135-7* $24.95
The Autobiography of Benjamin Franklin has probably been more extensively read than any other American historical work, and no other book of its kind has had such ups and downs of fortune. Franklin lived for many years in England, where he was agent... Biographies/History Pages 332

Name	
Email	
Telephone	
Address	
City, State ZIP	

☐ **Credit Card**   ☐ **Check / Money Order**

Credit Card Number	
Expiration Date	
Signature	

Please Mail to: Book Jungle
PO Box 2226
Champaign, IL 61825
or Fax to: 630-214-0564

ORDERING INFORMATION

web: *www.bookjungle.com*
email: *sales@bookjungle.com*
fax: *630-214-0564*
mail: *Book Jungle PO Box 2226 Champaign, IL 61825*
or PayPal *to sales@bookjungle.com*

Please contact us for bulk discounts

DIRECT-ORDER TERMS

**20% Discount if You Order
Two or More Books**
Free Domestic Shipping!
Accepted: Master Card, Visa,
Discover, American Express